The

Treasure Thief

By

Terri Daneshyar

First published in 2019

www.terridaneshyar.com
cover design by Leo Hartas
Illustrations by sharpesketch.com

ISBN-10: 9781706685296

Contents

Detention

The history classroom was warm, the sun shone directly onto Lottie sat at her desk in the back row. Her thoughts drifted away, across the school playing field and far beyond, to ancient Rome. She imagined herself, helmet pushed down over her mop of auburn hair, amongst the gladiators entering the arena to face wild beasts in a fight to the death. Ferocious cries and howls filled the air as the bravest and strongest men and beasts

1

grappled with each other in an epic battle of survival. In the background, Mrs Barclay, dressed as ever in a pale blue twin-set, horn-rimmed spectacles balancing precariously on the end of her nose, droned on and on about English monarchs, like the annoying buzz of a persistent fly.

'Charlotte Evans. Charlotte Evans. Stand up!'

Lottie snapped out of her daydream, hazel eyes glaring defiantly at Mrs Barclay and stood.

'Charlotte, you will recite the Kings and Queens of England from Charles II to the present day.'

It took a moment for Lottie to get her bearings and then she began, but her head was too full of gladiators to recall a list of dates. Give her a Roman coin or a piece of Greek marble and she could tell you it's entire story, but a list of dry dates just would not stick. Mrs Barclay slammed her ruler down on the desk.

'Detention. My room at 4pm, where you will write out the full list of monarchs.'

'But it's the last day of term!'

'Detention! Perhaps that will encourage you to pay more attention in class. You can't even get the date correct in your exercise book. It is 1966, not 266 BC. The Romans have no place in this lesson. Now, sit.'

Perhaps if your lessons weren't so dull, I might pay more attention, thought Lottie. It wasn't that she disliked history: she loved it. Growing up with an archaeologist father in a house full of ancient artefacts, history had always felt alive. Mrs Barclay managed to suck all of the enjoyment out of it and turn it into dust.

Later that day as she wandered along the corridor on the way to her detention, excited laughter from the dorms and the sound of trunks being closed, reminded her that school finished

3

for summer tomorrow. Lottie enjoyed boarding school now, with its camaraderie and routines. It hadn't always been like that. When she first arrived four years ago, she had felt very differently. Her mother had just died and her father, unable to deal with his grief and an eight-year old daughter, had shipped her off to Broadlands School for Girls, thinking that an all-female environment would be better for her now that her mother was gone. Poor Lottie, she felt like she had lost both parents. All she really wanted was to be at home in familiar surroundings that reminded her of her mum, not this strange and alien place with its shared dormitories and lack of privacy. Fortunately, she had a very kind and caring house mistress who had nurtured her through the first term and helped her settle in, until her natural bubbly and exuberant personality had opened up again. Once that happened, she fully embraced life at Broadlands and thrived, making friends, joining clubs and even organising secret dorm parties.

Now it was holidays, one last detention, then eight weeks with Papa. It cheered her up on the slow walk to do her punishment. Despite her father being an archaeology professor and often away on digs, he always made sure that he was home for the long summer holidays to spend them with her.

'History has lain where it is for thousands of years,' he said. 'It can wait a few more weeks for me.'

Summers with Lottie were non-negotiable, no matter what ancient treasure hunt he was working on. And what fun they were! They set each other puzzles and riddles to solve, tied rope into impossible knots and worked out how to undo them. He would hide clues around the house that led to hidden treasures. She would describe artefacts and he had to say what, when and where they were from. One of his more memorable puzzles had taken her all around the house and garden and down the lane to a neighbour's house where a surprise birthday party was waiting for her. Once she asked him why he was an archaeologist. He said, 'Archaeology is one big puzzle. If you followed the clues you could work out what it was telling you, and because I've always loved puzzles and history, it was the right job for me.'

She turned the corner to the history corridor and jumped at the touch of a hand on her shoulder.

A small girl with long dark plaits, stepped out of the shadows.

'Diana.'

'Here,' she whispered, slipping Lottie a folded note. 'I wrote the dates for you. Don't let Boring Barclay see.'

'Thank you,' smiled Lottie.

'That's what best friends are for,' said Diana, disappearing around the corner just as Mrs Barclay opened the door to her study.

'Take a seat Miss Evans. I trust you have brought your brain with you.'

She placed a sheet of lined paper on a small desk facing the wall.

'Sit!'

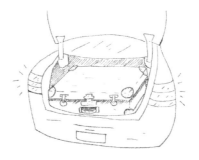

Aunt Helen

All the next day Broadlands Boarding School for Girls was filled with the excited chatter of girls and parents greeting each other. Hugs, smiles, gasps of astonishment at changes in height were echoing through the halls. Trunks were loaded, car boots slammed, engines revved, taking their happy passengers away from Latin, algebra, English grammar and French verbs for eight whole weeks of relaxation and family time.

Lottie's dorm, emptied of its other occupants, reverberated to the sound of her fingers drumming on the windowsill. *Papa's late.* She recalled the end of the summer two years ago when he had been setting off to his new position as visiting Professor of Archaeology at the American University of Beirut. This was a prestigious appointment. It was hard to tell who was the most nervous, him or her. Although her father was used to travelling, this was his first long stint away since Lottie's mother had died. Lottie smiled up at her father and thought how clever and strong he must be to go and live in a new country, not realising how worried he had been about leaving without his wife, who had always made him feel braver than he actually was, or how worried he was about Lottie.

I mustn't show him I don't want him to go, she thought. *I must be brave too.*

And she was brave. He had dropped her at school as usual at the start of the autumn term, squeezed her especially tightly and left, promising to write as soon as he got there. She didn't cry one tear until he was out of sight and couldn't see how devastated she was. A few weeks later, she received a newspaper cutting from Lebanon with a photograph of him and another very serious looking man. The article was about her father's appointment to the university in Beirut and said that Dr Baramki, the director of the university's museum, welcomed Professor Evans and hoped that he would enjoy his time in this cosmopolitan city. Lottie cut out the picture and tucked it into her pocket notebook that went everywhere with her, with a note explaining what cosmopolitan meant.

The crunch of gravel alerted her to the arrival of another car. She jumped down from the sill and looked out, but it wasn't for her. The portly shape and smiling face of Mr Florsham, father of Alice, who shared her dorm, stepped out of the vehicle. The room was quiet now. Silence had replaced the excited chatter of earlier. Sitting slumped forward on her trunk, chin resting on her hands, she waited. Patience was not her strong suit and with no company, time dragged on and on. By six o'clock it was clear something had seriously delayed Papa. At seven, she was summoned to the head's office.

Sitting in front of the headmistress's desk, Lottie saw an upright woman in a grey suit, blonde hair pulled back into the severest of buns. Feet, wearing sensible flat shoes, were crossed neatly at the ankle. The figure was so stiff that even the air around her seemed to have hardened.

'Aunt Helen?' said Lottie, puzzled.

Aunt Helen barely acknowledged her and carried on talking to the head. Lottie sat in the spare chair, a knot of anxiety forming in her stomach.

'Where is Papa?' she asked.

'Charlotte dear, your father has been … delayed and is unable to collect you. Your Aunt Helen will be taking you for the summer,' said Miss Reeve.

'But Papa always comes. He never misses the summer holidays.'

Aunt Helen turned to her,

'It could not be avoided, Charlotte. Now please don't fuss. All the arrangements have been made. We will be going to your home rather than mine to make it a little easier for you, but you are to be in my charge for the duration of the summer holidays. I trust you are packed and ready?'

Lottie nodded miserably and blinked back the tears that were forming, determined not to cry in front of her austere Aunt.

'Very well. Come along now.'

Aunt Helen stood and shook Miss Reeve's hand.

'Thank you for your understanding of the situation.'

She left the office, Lottie following slowly behind, her mind full of questions. The porters loaded her trunk and she climbed into Aunt Helen's car and stared miserably out of the window. There was no conversation. If Lottie did try to ask anything Aunt Helen raised her hand from the steering wheel to silence her. Never had the hour and a half journey home felt so long. Finally, the sight of the familiar Warwickshire roads cheered her up. Signposts for Stratford Upon Avon relaxed her a little. They passed through Henley in Arden with its delicious ice cream parlour, and on until they reached Mappley Village and the lane that led to Pinetops.

At least I'll be at home she thought looking at the familiar line of pine trees that guarded the front drive. The black and white gables of the house finally drew a smile from her. The heavy oak door was wide open and the comforting figure of Mrs Button the housekeeper, was there to greet her. Lottie flung open the car door and raced across the gravel into her arms. For the first time that day, Lottie felt the warmth of human contact. Mrs Button's hugs were huge and sincere and just what she needed. The smell of freshly baked bread wafted gently through the doorway, swiftly followed by the aroma of beef stew.

'Dumplings?' she asked.

'Naturally,' replied Mrs Button, 'It's your first day home.'

It may have been summer, but beef stew and dumplings with fresh bread was always the first home-cooked meal that Lottie and her father shared, being the firm favourite of them both.

Noticing her change of expression Mrs Button said, 'It's all right love. He would expect you to have it to celebrate being home. Come on in. I'll get Mr Button to unload your trunk while you eat, and you can tell me all about school and what you and Miss Diana have got up to this year.'

Lottie ran down the hall, past Papa's study with its shelves bulging with books and artefacts and into the familiar kitchen with its yellow stove and pale blue cupboards. There, on the round pine table, was a large brown casserole dish of beef stew, next to a freshly baked cottage loaf. Mrs Button served up a large bowlful and cut a few slices of bread, which she lathered in butter, before sitting down next to Lottie to hear all about school. Aunt Helen did not appear, preferring to eat on her own later when she had finished some work she had to do.

'Still keeps her own company I see,' said Mrs Button to Lottie. 'She's a closed book that one. Very private, not like your dad.'

'I prefer it being just us,' said Lottie. 'She makes me feel awkward.'

'I know what you mean, lass,' smiled Mrs Button. 'Now tuck in and tell me all about last term.'

The next morning Aunt Helen was waiting for Lottie in her father's study. His shelves of history books interspersed with clay pots or cases of bronze coins, even the odd marble bust, lined the walls of this, Lottie's favourite room in the house. The large mahogany desk with its untidy mess of papers spoke to her of the Roman forum or a Greek tragedy. *Papa,* she smiled to herself, only it wasn't Papa, it was her prim and proper Aunt Helen who sat behind the desk this morning, looking as out of place as a wooden bowl on a table of fine china.

'Do sit down, Charlotte. I have something important to tell you.'

'My name is Lottie,' she replied, slumping into the red leather armchair in the corner.

'Please do try to sit like a young lady, Charlotte, and not a lump of meat.'

'It's Lottie.'

Ignoring her, Aunt Helen continued.

'Your father has been … detained in Lebanon, so I have decided that the best course of action would be for us to go there and find … meet him.'

Lottie sat up.

'You mean actually go to where he works? To another country?'

'Yes, Charlotte.'

'How would we get there? Do we go by boat?'

'Charlotte my dear, for the daughter of a respected professor you seem to lead a very sheltered life. No. This is 1966. We will fly.'

Lottie's head whirred with possibilities. *An aeroplane. A real aeroplane. I'll be the envy of everyone at school. But Lebanon –* she remembered looking it up when her father took the position. She knew that it was on the Mediterranean near to Cyprus, and that it was an important centre for archaeology with its Phoenician roots and Turkish links, but beyond that she knew little about it. She had hardly enquired when Papa told her he would be working there for five years, only checking that he would still be home for the summer as usual.

'I promise you my darling,' her father had said before he left, 'I will be home for summer and hopefully Christmas too. They were my conditions when I was offered the post. I'm afraid you may have to spend the Easter holidays at school. I know five years seems a long time, but it will go quickly, and this is an important position, helping Dr Baramki expand the university's museum. He wants to make it a museum of archaeology, and there is a dig at a site in Byblos which we are hoping will unearth more Phoenician treasure.'

'Papa, it's fine. I know that your work is important,' she had replied, but she couldn't hide the disappointment in her voice. 'I don't mind Easters at school, just as long as you promise to be home for the summer.'

'My darling, try stopping me. I will write regularly and telephone too.'

And that is what he had done for the last two years. She had missed his weekend visits at first, but it was surprising how quickly she had adjusted. Although she had secretly hoped he wouldn't like it over there and come back early, deep down she knew that she would just have to wait five years.

Aunt Helen continued, and Lottie realised that she hadn't been paying attention.

'The official language is Arabic, but it is a former French colony, so they speak French too; and because of the number of visitors, they also speak a little English. No need to worry, you will manage quite adequately. I think you will find it a very interesting place. And for the sake of your manners, the Arabic for thank you is *Sucran.*'

'Cosmopolitan,' said Lottie. 'It means it has people from lots of different countries.'

'Yes, I know what it means,' said Aunt Helen, slightly irritated at being interrupted. 'We leave on Monday. You have the weekend to pack. It will be very hot there, so only take light clothes and a sun hat.'

'Shorts and tee shirts then. How long will we be there?'

'That is unclear at the moment, but I anticipate it will be for the majority of the summer.'

The conversation appeared to be over. Grabbing a book of maps to plot the flight, Lottie headed straight for her room. *Going to Lebanon, and on an aeroplane no less, meeting Papa at his place of work – perhaps the summer won't be so bad after all.*

Lottie takes a plane

On Monday morning Lottie and Aunt Helen set off in the car for London Heathrow Airport. It was a similar journey to their last one in that Aunt Helen didn't want any conversation. This time though, Lottie felt much more upbeat and excited for what was ahead.

'We fly to Orly Airport in Paris and from there we will get our connecting flight to Beirut,' said Aunt Helen, when they arrived.

'So, we go on two aeroplanes?'

'Yes Charlotte, we do,' said Aunt Helen, so matter of factly, that she made air travel seem like something quite mundane.

Heathrow was busy with fellow travellers. Porters pushing trolleys assisted with suitcases. Helpful people in very smart uniforms were showing travellers where they needed to go. Overhead signs had the names of destinations Lottie had only vague knowledge of, Istanbul, Majorca, Barcelona. The noise and excited chatter reminded Lottie of the first day of term when returning boarders mixed with new girls, a combination of those who strode around confidently, knowing their environment, and those for whom it was all new and strange. Lottie felt like a new girl all over again in this alien place, searching for something familiar to bring some comfort. Then she heard it: a sharp *clack clacking* of heels on a hard floor, and she thought for a moment that it was her headmistress approaching. Turning in the direction of the sound, she saw four immaculately dressed women in dark blue skirt suits, followed by three men in even smarter uniforms. It felt like time was suspended as these superior beings marched through passport control and on towards the departure gates. Everyone held their breath and watched in admiration, imagining themselves as pilots or glamorous stewardesses. Only Aunt Helen was unmoved by the scene as she continued to bustle Lottie past the passport window and on to the plane.

Lottie was bursting with anticipation. How fast did the plane fly? How high? Would it be smooth or bumpy? Might she feel sick? So many questions, prompting a rather impatient man behind them to say that there really ought to be a separate aeroplane for annoying children so that the adults could enjoy a peaceful flight.

Lottie's cheeks burned with anger and embarrassment. To her surprise, Aunt Helen turned around and severely chastised him.

'Sir, if all adults were like you and constantly quashing young, enquiring minds then we would still be living in the dark ages. We should be encouraging our children to learn, not shoving them in corners to be forgotten.'

He was so shocked to be put firmly in his place, that he ceased complaining and took his seat without further comment. Lottie could have hugged Aunt Helen, but the look in her eye made it quite clear that it was neither necessary nor appropriate. However, she did offer Lottie the window seat, which she accepted enthusiastically.

Once everyone was seated, the stewardesses told them all what to do in an emergency and where to find the exits. Lottie listened attentively and even took notes.

'I'm sure that isn't necessary my dear,' said Aunt Helen. 'If we do have a problem you are not going to have time to consult your notebook.'

'I know, but I want to remember what she said and look, I've a diagram of the plane so that I can study it again once we are airborne.'

Airborne, thought Lottie. *I can't believe it. I wish Papa was here to share this with me.* Before she had time to slip into melancholy the plane began taxiing towards the runway. The engines roared and suddenly they were moving at breakneck speed and then gosh, oh gosh, they lifted off the ground. The higher they climbed, the smaller the people and buildings below became. Pressure built up in Lottie's ears and then released itself with a pop. The plane passed through a cloud and began to shake. The captain's voice came over the tannoy apologising for the slight turbulence. All the adults, including Aunt Helen, were clutching tightly to the arms of their seats, knuckles white. But Lottie wasn't scared; it was all part of the thrill of being in a plane.

As soon as the turbulence passed, the stewardesses came round offering them drinks and snacks. Aunt Helen ordered a lemonade for Lottie and a tea for herself.

Lemonade at twenty thousand feet tastes better than ever, thought Lottie, as she sat back staring at the blue sky and listening to the roar of the engines. *I can't wait to tell Diana.*

In what seemed like a very short time she felt them begin to descend. Amazingly the stewardesses came round with bags of boiled sweets for the passengers. Lottie looked at Aunt Helen who nodded at her to take one.

'It's to relieve the pressure as we land,' she said.

A loud clunk indicated that the landing gear had been deployed, then there was a heavy thud and juddering as the plane hit the runway and the pilot applied the brakes. Now it was Lottie's turn to be gripping the seat. The plane slowed and turned, and Orly Airport came into view.

They disembarked quickly and Aunt Helen rushed her through the airport to find their connecting flight.

'What about our suitcases?'

'Don't worry about them, the baggage handlers will see that they get to our plane.'

Lottie wasn't convinced about this but Aunt Helen spoke with such authority it was pointless to worry.

The second plane was even bigger than the first and the roar of the engines at take-off was twice as loud, but Lottie didn't mind, it was just so exciting. This time they were given a proper meal, an omelette, French cheese, bread and a very sweet and sticky cake. The cheese, called camembert, smelt so strong that Lottie thought it had gone off, but watching Aunt Helen tuck in, she decided to give it a try. *If I am going to a new country, I must try new tastes,* she thought. The sharp tang as it hit her tongue was surprisingly good and she finished it off in no time.

When the trays had been removed, Lottie sat back and looked out of the window. *Lebanon,* she thought. *I wonder what it will be like? It must be okay if Papa is there. He wouldn't go somewhere dangerous or horrible. But why isn't he home? What did Aunt Helen say, he had been delayed? That didn't sound like Papa.* A knot of unease formed in her stomach. She took the newspaper photograph out of her notebook. Her father's smiling face looked back at her. *Please be okay.* Aunt Helen noticed the picture and laid a reassuring hand on her arm.

'I'm sure your father will soon be with us. Once he has finished his university business.'

Lottie thought she detected a note of hesitation in Aunt Helen's voice, which unsettled her even more.

'Maybe he'll be at the airport waiting for us,' said Lottie with a false air of cheeriness.

'We shall see,' replied Aunt Helen.

Lottie folded up the newspaper cutting and put it carefully back inside her notebook, sat back and stared out of the window, her head full of Papa. The next thing she knew, Aunt Helen was gently shaking her.

'Charlotte, Charlotte dear, we've landed. Time to disembark.'

Shaking herself awake, Lottie walked rather sluggishly to the exit. A wall of heat hit her as she walked through the aeroplane door and down the steps.

'Welcome to Lebanon and thank you for flying with us,' said the stewardess as Lottie followed

Aunt Helen across the scorching tarmac and into
Beirut International Airport's arrivals building.

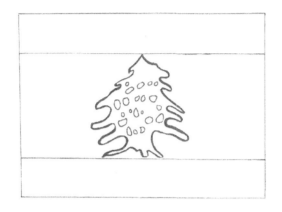

Lebanon

The airport was noisy and chaotic. People jostled for position in the queue for passport control. Raised voices in a foreign tongue sounding so alien to Lottie. Arm waving and gesticulating only added to the general chaos. Feeling more than a little lost and overwhelmed, Lottie stuck close to Aunt Helen who remained her prim and proper self. The heat clung to Lottie like a heavy blanket, weighing her down and draining her energy. *How does she do it?* thought Lottie, watching Aunt Helen in her crisply tailored suit, negotiate the throng without even breaking sweat.

As if reading her thoughts Aunt Helen said, 'I'm used to travelling. Come along, we need this line.'

Peeling off from the main herd, she led them through the 'Channel Diplomatique', showed their passports and visas, then hurried them on to the baggage carousels to reclaim their luggage.

'Ooh there's mine,' squealed Lottie, delighted to be reunited with her suitcase.

A helpful porter lifted the case onto a trolley for her and when Aunt Helen's appeared shortly after, they made their way outside to find a taxi.

If the airport was confusing, the roads were even more so. Cars jumped lanes without indicating and horns honked relentlessly, as drivers jostled with each other for road position. Although not well versed in the rules of driving, Lottie felt sure that in England the roads had set lanes and you stopped at junctions, here everyone just kept pushing forward. On more than a few occasions their driver swerved violently to miss a car that had just decided to pull out in front of them. All of this was played out to a symphony of horns.

'I think if they took away the car horns the traffic would stop,' said Lottie. 'They don't seem to be able to move without honking them.'

Aunt Helen looked at her, and just for a second allowed the corners of her mouth to curl up into smile.

'This is just how it is here Charlotte. One does get used to it.'

'I'm not sure I shall,' said Lottie as their driver went head to head with an oncoming taxi, only to turn at the very last moment to avoid a collision.

The taxi pulled up outside the Hotel Excelsior, a very modern, high rise building and one of the newest in Beirut. Lottie's jaw dropped as she gazed in awe at the tall structure in front of her. The ten-storey building of clean white concrete was unlike anything she had seen before. They entered the lobby, its polished marble floor gleaming with pride. Looking through the glass doors at the rear she could see palm trees.

'Go and look while I check us in. It will probably take about ten minutes. I will wait just over there for you,' said Aunt Helen, pointing to a white leather settee, positioned so carefully that its occupants had full view of both the street and garden entrance.

Lottie disappeared through the rear doors and stepped into paradise. Carefully sculpted rhododendrons, bright scarlet and purple bougainvillea, tall palm trees, manicured shrubs and, artfully positioned amidst the greenery, white and orange tables shaded by large umbrellas, where guests could sit and relax. At the sound of a splash, Lottie spun around – but her view was blocked by a particularly large shrub. Taking a few steps around it, her heart leapt with joy as she gazed on the rippling blue water of the hotel swimming pool. This was too much for Lottie and she raced back to Aunt Helen. Forgetting all her manners, she dragged her aunt outside.

'You must see this. It's amazing! Are we really staying here? Can I use it?'

'Use what Charlotte?'

'This,' said Lottie, pointing delightedly at the swimming pool.

'Of course, my dear. Why do you think I chose this hotel? I thought you would need a distraction while we wait for your father.'

'Aunt Helen, I could kiss you,' said Lottie.

'That will not be necessary Charlotte,' replied Aunt Helen a little uncomfortably. 'But I am glad you like it. Now we must head up to our room and unpack.'

The room was enormous. Lottie tried one of the beds, rolling from side to side and bouncing on it to test it.

'This is much more comfy than the beds at school.'

'That's marvellous, Charlotte, but would you mind being a little less bouncy and get on with your unpacking?'

Lottie opened her suitcase and spilled its contents onto the bed, before pulling open the wardrobe.

'Oh look, there's a mini kettle with tea and coffee. I wish we could have one of these in the dorm. And there's an ironing board and iron! That's funny. I wouldn't want one of those at school. Imagine having to do your own ironing!'

Aunt Helen tutted loudly. Looking at her in her crisp, neat clothes Lottie thought that ironing was probably her favourite hobby. Something whirred and the air in the room began to cool.

'Air conditioning,' said Aunt Helen.

'What a marvellous machine,' said Lottie as the room temperature dropped to something more comfortable. 'I think I am going to like Lebanon.'

They had dinner in the hotel restaurant where French and American accents mixed with the Arabic. The waiting staff spoke all three languages. Lottie felt rather ashamed that she could only manage one and a half. More like one and a quarter really, she thought, remembering how little attention she paid in French lessons. Papa had always tried to drum into her how valuable it is to be able to speak in other languages.

'Not only is it a sign of respect when you visit another country,' her father had said, 'It also makes travelling and working abroad so much easier. It opens up so many opportunities for you.'

'But you never take me anywhere and I hate Miss Howard, so what is the point?'

'One day darling girl, I promise I will take you with me, so you'd better practise those French verbs.'

I should have listened to you Papa. My French is atrocious. She resolved to ask Aunt Helen to buy her a French phrase book to help her improve.

After dinner, Aunt Helen said she should go straight to bed.

'But it's only nine o'clock!'

'Actually, it is eleven o'clock. Lebanon is two hours ahead of England.'

'But I'm not tired, and it's holidays.'

'Nevertheless, bed it is. It will be a late evening tomorrow.'

Honestly, thought Lottie, *you are worse than matron. Papa would not make me go to bed.* She knew there was no point arguing further so she did as she was told. Despite her protests, the travelling had tired her out and she was asleep five minutes after climbing into bed.

Once Lottie was under, Aunt Helen opened her black attaché case, that she carried everywhere with her and removed some papers. Amongst them was a list of names with brief biographies, giving details of the individuals. While she studied the list, a large envelope was pushed under the door. Checking that Lottie was still asleep, Aunt Helen walked over and retrieved the envelope. It contained photographs of an ancient Greek marble sculpture and some information on its value and history. After studying its contents carefully, she placed them into the case, locked it and retired to bed.

Lace and ribbons

When Lottie woke up the next morning, she found a breakfast tray on the table loaded with croissants, orange juice, bread and cheese. There was also a note from Aunt Helen saying she had business to attend to, and that Charlotte was to amuse herself in the hotel complex until she returned. Written in capitals was the warning; UNDER NO CIRCUMSTANCES LEAVE THE HOTEL. Ordinarily that would have been an invitation to do the exact opposite, but this morning Lottie had just one thing on her mind. Swimming.

She wolfed down breakfast, put on her swimsuit and a tee shirt, grabbed a towel and the bottle of sun lotion Aunt Helen had thoughtfully left on the table, and raced downstairs to throw herself into the gloriously inviting water. The sun beds were all occupied and Lottie smiled as she watched the women taking care to get exactly the right amount of skin exposed, so there were no strap lines in their tan. A couple of teenage girls were painting each other's nails. Lottie grinned, remembering the time Diana had tried to paint her nails, but she hadn't been able to sit still long enough for the polish to dry.

'Why do people bother with all this? It's far too much effort.'

'Because Lottie,' replied Diana, 'Some of us want to look more feminine.'

Lottie burst out laughing. 'Can you imagine me being feminine? Diana you are funny. I'd much rather be outdoors. You are the girly one not me.'

Diana sighed, 'I guess you're right. Maybe one day we'll get you in a dress.'

'Never,' beamed Lottie.

The memory faded and still smiling to herself, Lottie dived into the water.

Having joyfully spent most of the day in the pool, she opened the hotel room and recoiled in horror at the pile of white lace and pink ribbon adorning her bed.

'What is that?'

'That, Charlotte, is a rather expensive dress that I have just bought for you. We have been invited to a party at The Grand Hotel de l'Orient this evening, and we must dress appropriately.'

Lottie picked up the pile of lace and wondered when on earth it could possibly be appropriate for her to wear such a hideous creation.

'But Aunt Helen, I never wear dresses. Papa would never ever make me wear anything like this.'

'Well, your father isn't here. I am your official guardian for the present, so you will wear the dress and try to look and behave like a young lady rather than…'

Aunt Helen looked at the wet tee shirt and dirty feet and the tousled mop of red hair, dripping onto the carpet.

'Rather than what?' demanded Lottie.

'Rather than an untidy mess. I shall run you a bath and you can wash the chlorine out of your hair and make yourself presentable.'

'I'm not wearing it. It's horrible!'

'Charlotte you will do as you are told. Your father is far too lenient with you. You have inherited his stubborn streak. And if you keep pulling that awful face you will end up with frown lines.'

The scent of bubble bath wafted gently into the bedroom. Catching sight of herself in the mirror, Lottie realised how dishevelled she looked. Her skin smelt of chlorine and her feet were filthy. With slow steps and slumped shoulders, she entered the bathroom.

Lottie could not remember feeling more uncomfortable in her entire life. The lace sleeves were itchy, the white collar was stiff and reflected light up onto her face emphasising her freckles, which had come out in full force after a day of sunshine and swimming. The wide pink sash at her waist had been pulled so tight by Aunt Helen that she could hardly breathe, and the pink ballet pumps pinched her toes. She was in a thoroughly bad mood and sulked all the way to the party.

'Do try to smile, Charlotte. We are going to meet some important people who know your father.'

Mention of her Papa perked her up a little, but as they entered the sumptuous hotel, a glance in the mirror at the large meringue shape she saw reflected, meant she retreated back into her sulk.

The party was a truly lavish affair, full of local dignitaries. She was introduced to General Haddad, the Chief of Police and his glamourous wife, who, dripping in gold, constantly stopped and admired herself in any mirror she passed. Then Lottie met Dr Dimitri Baramki, the Director of The Museum of Archaeology at The American University of Beirut, where her father worked.

'I'm very pleased to meet you, my dear. Your father is working on a very important site for us. His discoveries will really enhance the museums reputation. You must be very proud of him.'

'Yes, yes, I am,' said Lottie. 'Do you know when he will be finished? I can't wait to see him.'

'Ah no, I am not sure when that will be.'

Flustered by her question, he excused himself from the conversation. *Odd,* thought Lottie stifling a yawn. She peeled away from Aunt Helen and sat down on a golden seat with plush velvet cushions and surveyed the scene. A large table was laid out with all manner of interesting foods, bright green salads, tight green leaf parcels, little pastries stuffed with meat or cheese, jewelled rice, creamy spreads, huge slices of bright red tomatoes and bowls of black and green olives. It all looked delicious, but she was so uncomfortable in her lacy dress that she didn't feel like eating.

There was another girl in the room similar in age to herself, whose hair fell in perfectly coiled ringlets. Her blue dress sat neatly on slim shoulders and she appeared completely at ease in its frills and lace. Unlike Lottie, who was far more comfortable in dungarees or shorts, this girl looked like an exquisite china doll, the sort you find in expensive country houses, designed to be admired, not played with. She had an air of someone who was used to admiration and praise. Lottie sighed, then spotted Aunt Helen deep in conversation with a man in a very expensive suit, his dark hair slicked back perfectly and held in place by some kind of oil with a sheen matched only by his shoes which were so highly polished they sparkled when the light hit them. Lottie decided to wander over.

'It is very important that the Professor's notes are found. I am paying a large sum of money to the university, and I expect results.'

He was about to continue when he realised that Lottie was standing beside them. His manner immediately changed.

'Ah, you must be Professor Evans' daughter. Charlotte, isn't it?' he said offering his hand in greeting. 'I am Count Zindani.'

'It's Lottie,' she replied, feeling the tight grip of the Count's long fingers around her hand. 'I'm only called Charlotte when I'm in trouble.'

'Charlotte, it is a pleasure to meet you. I am a great admirer of your father.'

'What did you mean about finding Papa's notes? Has something happened to him?'

'Not at all, my dear. We have just… mislaid a notebook of his. Nothing to worry about.'

'But he's very careful with his notebooks. If one is missing something must be wrong.'

'Now Charlotte, dear, let's not get carried away. I expect it simply got lost in transit. The postal system here is not quite the same as in England,' said Aunt Helen.

'Indeed, indeed. I expect that is what has happened,' said the Count, but there was an underlying menace to his voice that made Lottie shiver.

Lottie was unconvinced. She knew her father and he would not have misplaced a notebook, but as neither of the grown-ups had anything more to say on the subject, she left them to their conversation. There was something about the Count that she didn't like. Whether it was the way he looked down his long nose at her, the sharp black eyes or his general demeanour she wasn't sure, but she resolved to find out more about him.

The girl with the ringlets came over to talk to her.

'Hi, I'm Eleanor. My father is the American Ambassador.'

'Lottie,' said Lottie

'Mother said to invite you to join us.'

Lottie looked across at the group of Americans all immaculately dressed and perfectly poised.

'That's kind of you,' said Lottie, remembering her manners, 'But I've just seen a friend of my father's. Perhaps later.'

Eleanor shrugged, looking slightly relieved at not having to spend time and make forced conversation with this stranger. She returned to her parents.

Lottie headed to the bathrooms where she furiously undid the pink sash and dumped it in the bin before flopping into a chair by the open window. The sounds of conversations in a foreign tongue and the incessant honking of car horns, drifted upwards from the streets and she wondered what it was like outside. When the smell of fresh coffee caught her nostrils she jumped up, decision made.

Finding her way out on to the street would be easy enough, but she didn't want the grand sweeping entrance to the hotel she wanted the back door with its mean streets and real people, not pompous party guests. A young waiter headed down a side corridor and she followed, watching him open a fire exit and sneak out. She did the same, walking out onto a narrow residential street. Already the sounds were drawing her closer. Lottie gave no thought to being alone in a foreign country and let her reckless curiosity lead her on. Despite it being nine o'clock at night, the cafes and shops were bustling. It felt more like mid-morning than mid-evening, with lively conversation everywhere. Outside the cafes, men were smoking from long pipes attached to tall glass bottles with round bulbous bottoms and small eggcup shaped chimneys on top holding burning charcoal. The air was full of the smoke from the fruited tobaccos they used.

'They are called nargile, or hubble bubbles because of the bubbles at the bottom when they suck on the pipe. See?'

She looked at the bottles and then at the boy who was talking to her. He was probably a similar age to her, dressed simply in slightly grubby jeans and a tee shirt. Something about his smile made her feel that she could trust him.

'I'm Amir,' he said.

'Lottie.'

'Where are you from?'

'England – I'm here with my Aunt. My father works at the University. We've come to meet him.'

'Welcome to Beirut, Lottie. Nice dress.'

'It's hideous. I hate it.'

'Then why are you wearing it?'

Lottie pointed behind her. 'My Aunt. Fancy party, very boring.'

Amir nodded sympathetically. 'I bet the food looks amazing, but no one is eating it.'

Lottie nodded, 'I think they are all afraid to make a mess.'

'Are you hungry?'

Lottie realised that she hadn't eaten since breakfast and her tummy rumbled.

'Famished,' she said.

'Come with me,' said Amir, grabbing her hand and pulling her down the road. She thought they would go to one of the cafes, but instead he took her down a narrow side street, through an alleyway, then down some steps to another wider street. He stopped at a small shop that had a contraption that looked like an upturned bowl at the front.

'Kefic Mahmood, *(how are you)*' called Amir.

An elderly man, with dark swarthy skin full of crinkles, appeared from the inside. His eyes smiled in greeting when he saw Amir.

'This is Lottie, and she is very hungry.'

Lottie held out her hand, but the man placed his on his heart and nodded politely at her. She wasn't sure what to make of this but decided it was best to nod in return.

'Two of your finest *saj* please,' said Amir, 'With cheese, tomato and olives.'

Lottie watched as the old man took two flat, round pieces of bread and put them on the upturned bowl, which was actually a hot stone. He then put slices of cheese on top and let the bread cook through and the cheese melt. When it was ready, he lifted them off with a spatula and placed them on sheets of greaseproof paper before adding cucumber, tomato slices and olives. Then he rolled the whole thing up into a sausage shape and passed one to Lottie and one to Amir. Lottie looked at it in wonder and then bit into it hungrily. It was delicious. The tomatoes were full of flavour and the cheese had a distinctive salty tang which matched perfectly with a slightly bitter taste she didn't recognise but thought must be the olives.

Mahmood looked on with pride as this English girl in the lacy dress tucked in to his food.

'Thank you,' she said 'It's so good.'

'Sucran Habibe, (*thank you my friend*)' said Amir and dropped a few coins on the counter. Mahmood waved them away, but Amir insisted.

The children wandered off.

'This food is superb. I could eat it every day,' said Lottie.

'You could, but Lebanon has so many flavours you must try. Now we will get dessert.'

This time he stopped outside a shop whose window was full of little pastry parcels sprinkled with chopped nuts and icing sugar. Inside, the shelves were filled with boxes of these delicious morsels. A man in a long white tunic and baggy pants came forward. When he saw Amir, he broke into an enormous smile.

'Reza, this is my friend Lottie, from England. She would like to try a piece of your finest *bacclava* please.'

Reza indicated a stool for her to sit on, then Amir told her to close her eyes and open her mouth. When her eyes were tightly shut, Reza placed a small piece of the pastry on her tongue. With her mouth closed, the sweetness of the pastry, mixed with the pistachio nuts enfolded her taste buds. It was definitely the most glorious thing she had ever tasted. The pastry was so light and delicate it literally melted in her mouth, and its honey coating swamped her tongue in its deliciousness. She opened her eyes. Amir and Reza looked on expectantly.

'Exquisite. Amazing. Wonderful. That was the loveliest thing I have ever tasted.'

Reza clapped his hands in delight and made her up a box of the pastries to take with her. Amir tried to pay but Reza shook his head.

'The look of delight on the young lady's face when she tasted my *bacclava* is payment enough.'

Lottie thanked him over and over before Amir took her off to a corner café and found them seats in the back, where they sat huddled together like two conspirators. A waiter approached and placed a bowl of flat breads on the table. Amir ordered something in Arabic and a few moments later the waiter placed a bowl of hummus, two glasses and a jug of dark red liquid. Amir poured Lottie a glass. She sniffed it. Rose petals, she thought. It hit her tongue with a burst of refreshing sweetness.

'It's called *jalap*. Do you like it?'

'Delicious. How do you come to speak English so well?'

'We have to learn it in school. It's useful. So many Americans come here, some English too. But tell me how an English girl in a lacy dress is brave enough to be alone in Beirut?'

In all the excitement of the night's new flavours, Lottie had quite forgotten the dress.

'Oh no, Aunt Helen! Please can you get me back to the Orient Hotel? I'm for the high jump now.'

'What is high jump?' asked a very puzzled Amir.

'It means I'm in really big trouble.'

Amir knew what that felt like and led her through the kitchen and out the back of the café. Lottie wasn't given to panicking, but she had no idea how long she had been away from the party or just how mad Aunt Helen would be. Luckily Amir knew a quick route and got her back to the hotel in minutes. He snuck her back in through the rear entrance and then before she had time to thank him, disappeared into the night. She headed for the foyer where several policemen were questioning staff and guests. Lottie wandered over to the American girl with the ringlets and asked what was going on, even though she had a pretty good idea.

'I've found her! She's here,' shouted Eleanor.

Everyone turned around and Lottie felt a hundred pairs of eyes staring at her. Aunt Helen, seething with rage, marched over.

'Charlotte Evans, where on earth have you been? And look at the state of you! Have you been attacked?'

Lottie, cheeks burning, shook her head.

'I went for a walk.'

'On your own? In a strange country? Anything could have happened to you! Whatever possessed you to do such a reckless thing?'

'I was bored. And I wasn't alone. I met this boy called Amir and he showed me around.'

Hearing the name Amir, General Haddad approached.

'Amir did you say? Was he about your age and height? Green eyes?'

'Yes, and he was very kind,' said Lottie.

'Where is he now?'

'I don't know sir. He brought me back here and left.'

The General did not look at all pleased.

'Do you know this boy?' asked Aunt Helen.

'Yes, I'm afraid I do, but as the young lady is safe, I think that we should all retire. I will deal with the young man later.'

'It wasn't his fault,' said Lottie. 'And without him I would definitely have got lost.'

'That is quite enough out of you, young lady. You have spoilt everyone's evening. Now come along.'

The silence in the taxi was unbearable. Aunt Helen was furious and Lottie was ashamed of the fuss she had caused. Once in their room, the lacy dress was peeled off. Aunt Helen held it up in disgust, tutting at the state of it.

'Where is the sash?'

'I put it in the bin at the hotel.'

'What? Have you any idea how much this cost? It is completely ruined. I am disappointed in you Charlotte, causing so much upset and worry.'

Lottie couldn't get into bed quickly enough, wanting to bury her shame and guilt under the crisp white sheets.

Later, when Lottie was sleeping, Aunt Helen opened her attaché case and wrote a short note, which she handed to the night porter with strict instructions on where it needed to go.

Lottie makes a discovery

Lottie woke late and realised that Aunt Helen was missing again. There was no sign of the dress or the ballet pumps. Lottie ate the breakfast that had been left for her and got dressed in a tee shirt and shorts. A note lay on the desk, written in capitals ordering her to STAY PUT. She wandered to the window. Already the sun loungers were full, and waiters were busy taking drinks and snacks to their guests. Before a wave of self-pity could overwhelm her, Lottie decided to use the time to write to Diana. She sat at the table, picked up her pen and notebook, and began. Her words spilled out in a hurry, describing the airport, the flight, the view from the window, the boiled sweets, but most of all, the adventure of the previous evening:

Of course, I'm paying for it now, she wrote. *Matron has got me confined to barracks on pain of having to wear another pink lace monstrosity. It was so worth it though, Diana. The saj was really tasty, and those little pastries were heavenly. I will definitely bring some back for us to eat in the dorm. I might even give one to Boring Barclay. You never know, it might get me out of detention for a while.*

I hope I meet Amir again. I forgot to tell him where we are staying. I've got to do more exploring. Maybe we'll hear from Papa today. I really miss him and I'm starting to get very worried. I certainly don't like that Count, although Aunt Helen seems very pally with him.

I'll write again soon.

Your best friend,

Lottie

With the letter finished, she was about to risk going down to reception to find an envelope and ask if they could post it for her – but the sound of the key in the door put an end to that idea.

'Ah Charlotte, you are dressed. Good. We have a luncheon appointment. Come along.'

Without further explanation, Aunt Helen marched her out of the room and downstairs to a waiting car. Lottie let out a low whistle, prompting a glare from Aunt Helen.

'Charlotte, please don't be so vulgar.'

'But it's a Rolls Royce.'

'A Phantom V, to be exact,' said the driver proudly. 'Count Zindani's favourite.'

'I'm not surprised,' said Lottie admiring the sleek bodywork, the iconic metal grille and above it, the small figurine of the woman leaning forwards, arms outstretched, with a billowing cloth behind her, running from her arms to her back to resemble wings. Inside, the cream leather seats were sumptuous and extremely comfortable. The engine purred. Lottie noticed that the usually mad drivers held back in deference to this magnificent car. *This must be what royalty feels like,* she thought, waving imperiously at passing pedestrians. Aunt Helen appeared entirely unimpressed by this luxury vehicle, taking it in with the air of someone who rode in them all the time. *How on earth are you and Papa related?* thought Lottie.

The car took them out of Beirut and up into the mountains. The city's tower blocks and dusty streets fell away as the road snaked upwards. Tall cedar trees grew on the side of the mountain. Looking behind, Lottie could see the bay where the sparkling blue water of the Mediterranean smiled its welcome. On they drove to a place called Aley. It was a small town with the usual array of cafés and shops, but everything was much greener up here. Purple bougainvillea tumbled down walls, filling the roadside with bursts of colour. Lowering the window, Lottie inhaled the fresh mountain air mixed with the delicate fragrance of the jasmine that grew everywhere. It was cooler too, the altitude cutting through the heat with its fresh breeze.

The car pulled into a large compound in front of a five-storey building that looked like it grew out of the mountain. A collection of expensive cars, Porches, Ferraris, Bugattis, lined the perimeter and Lottie wondered what one individual could possibly want with so many vehicles. A young boy was busy polishing a silvery-blue porche, making its bodywork gleam like it belonged in a showroom.

The elaborate gold doors of the house were thrown open and a beaming Count Zindani burst through them.

'Good morning, ladies. Welcome to my humble home.'

There is nothing remotely humble about you or your home, thought Lottie, dutifully following Aunt Helen to greet their host. He took Aunt Helen's gloved hand and touched it gently to his lips. At the sight of this, Lottie shoved hers deep into the pockets of her shorts. Without appearing to notice, the Count ushered them into a marble hallway hung with ornate gold mirrors and lined with antique French side tables, which were adorned with vases of fresh flowers. He led them up the marble stairway to the first floor where he opened a pair of elegantly carved mahogany doors onto the largest sitting room Lottie had ever seen.

'Welcome to my salon. Please make yourself at home. I will order some refreshments. Tea perhaps?'

'That would be lovely,' said Aunt Helen. 'Charlotte dear, would you like tea or perhaps lemonade?'

But Lottie didn't answer; she was beguiled by the ancient treasures that filled the vast room.

'This is like your own personal museum,' she said. Everywhere she looked there was something to admire. A bronze life-size statue of a Roman soldier, a Ming vase, smaller Egyptian statuettes of the god Horus, display cabinets of ancient coins or jewellery. So much to see!

'I do possess many wonderful treasures. I also have pieces on loan at our National Museum and

The Louvre in Paris, but I like to keep my favourites here.'

'How did you get them?'

'My dear Charlotte, a gentleman does not like to brag, but I am a man of considerable wealth and when I am offered items… well let's just say, I like to collect.'

'I believe that you have also funded several archaeological digs, including the one my brother is currently working on,' said Aunt Helen.

'Why, yes. This one is for The American University of Beirut, for their Museum of Archaeology. It is important to support our academic institutions and the great work that they do, is it not? And Dr Baramki is extremely grateful for my assistance.'

Lottie thought that she detected the merest hint of a raised eyebrow from Aunt Helen at the Count's last remark.

'Have you heard anything from the Professor? I had rather hoped that your luncheon invitation was to pass on some news as to when we can expect his return.'

'I am afraid I have no updates,' said the Count.

Their conversation was interrupted by the butler informing them that luncheon was served.

Lottie stared open-mouthed at this unexpected entrance. Noticing her expression, the Count said, 'You seem a little surprised that I have a butler, my dear Charlotte. Why wouldn't I? A gentleman always relies on his butler. I'm sure it is the same in England.'

Lottie turned away, mimicking the Count's words under her breath.

Lunch was laid out in an equally sumptuous dining room, at a marble table bedecked with golden plates and cutlery. They sat on gold high-backed chairs and ate a delicious assortment of dishes while the Count regaled them with tales of his many trips around the world. Lottie only half listened: the pincer movements of his long slender fingers distracted her. They reminded her of the machines at fairgrounds with the claw that grabs prizes. She imagined the Count leaning over her father and grasping the treasures he unearthed with his claw-like hands. There was something slightly sinister about him, an underlying feeling that he felt himself superior to other people in every way, and the antiquities that he had acquired were his by right.

'Professor Evans has unearthed some significant Phoenician treasures on my current dig,' he said.

'You mean the University's dig,' corrected Aunt Helen.

'Yes, yes, of course, for the University,' said the Count, slightly irritated.

'Charlotte dear, why don't you go and study the Count's collection? If that is acceptable, Count? I'm sure our conversation will be somewhat tedious for you'

'Be my guest, Charlotte. Your Aunt and I have plenty to discuss'

Lottie made her way back to the main salon and mooched about amongst the treasures, enjoying the thrill of picking up a two-thousand-year-old figurine or coin, something strictly forbidden in museums. Naturally, she was extremely careful with them, understanding how fragile they were. The entire wall at the end of the room was a bookcase, filled with leather-bound volumes. Lottie ran her finger along the spines searching for something she might recognise, but the majority were in Arabic. Halfway along the third shelf was a spine with raised lettering. *Curious,* she thought, and tried to remove the book. It slid forward about half an inch and then wouldn't budge. Lottie knew immediately what it was. She pushed the book firmly back into position and, just as expected, a section of the bookcase swung outwards. With a swift check that no one had seen her, she stepped inside the room which had just been revealed. It was dark but after a quick feel along the wall she located a switch.

Looking around, she saw a large desk covered in papers. Maps lined the walls, many of them with location pins in them. On closer inspection she saw that they were all marked as archaeological sites. The papers on the desk were a mixture of receipts, letters and certificates of origin. One of them was headed 'Buyers' and underneath was a list of names and items.

Saif khalim – Egyptian mummy
Edward Manniger – Greek marble

Pierre Lestrange – Hieroglyphic tablet

Hans Merkal – Byblos statuettes

Sara McCall – Persian bronze

The list went on for two pages.

There was also a sheet of University headed paper. Lottie grabbed it eagerly and saw it was from Dr Baramki.

Dear Count Zindani

I am concerned that some of the items from the Byblos dig appear to have gone missing. The professor and his students assure me that every find has been catalogued, but when I last spoke to him the number of items he had sent and the number I received did not match up. Could you kindly look into this for me? I am sure that there is a simple explanation.

Kind regards,

Dr Baramki

Lottie heard her name being called and dashed out of the secret room, only remembering at the last second to turn off the light. Pressing the book to close the door, she sat on the floor with a volume of Arabic verse open in her lap, which is where the Count and her Aunt found her.

'There you are. Didn't you hear us call?'

Lottie looked up.

'Sorry Aunt Helen, I was looking at these books.'

'Do you read Arabic?' asked the Count, gently stroking the spines of the books to ensure they were all in place.

'Oh no, but I love the shape of the letters and I'm trying to find patterns. You have many interesting things,' said Lottie, looking straight at the Count.

'Well I am sorry Charlotte, but you must put the book back.' Aunt Helen gestured towards the door. 'It is time for us to leave.'

Lottie closed the book and replaced it. 'Thank you for letting me study your collection. It was very interesting.'

'I'm glad you thought so,' replied the Count.

'Oh yes, it was most informative,' she smiled at him.

The Count glared back at her.

Lottie followed Aunt Helen to the waiting car, the Count watching her all the way. Something about her manner made him suspicious. He went to his secret office behind the bookcase and checked his desk for any sign of intrusion. Everything looked to be in order, but then he noticed the letter from Dr Baramki was not quite where he had left it. He pressed a buzzer on the desk and in moments two heavy-set and menacing-looking men appeared.

'You will make sure to follow the Professor's daughter. She has been rifling through my personal papers. I want to know where she goes and who she meets.'

'Yes Sir,' they both said in unison.

'And Khalid, Hassan. Discretion, please.'

By the pool

'I'm not sure I like Count Zindani,' announced Lottie when they were safely back in their hotel room. 'Do you?'

'Whether I like him or not is no concern of yours,' said Aunt Helen. 'I have to go to the University. Can I trust you to remain here?'

'Can I go swimming please?'

'Yes, that's a good idea. You may order yourself some drinks and snacks and charge them to the room. Do not forget to apply sun lotion.'

'Yes Aunt Helen. Thank you.'

'Oh, and Charlotte?'

'Yes?'

'Stay within the hotel complex and out of trouble.'

'Yes Aunt Helen. I promise.'

'Good. Then I will see you at six o'clock.'

An afternoon on her own! Lottie pumped the air in delight. Five minutes later, swimming costume and sun screen on, she was on her way downstairs with Diana's letter in her hand.

'Please could you post this for me?' she asked the man at reception.

'Certainly Miss Evans. I also have a letter for you,' he replied, handing her a sheet of neatly folded paper. Intrigued, Lottie open the note.

Third table on the right by the pool.

She turned back to the receptionist to ask who it was from, but he was now occupied trying to check in a family of Americans for whom nothing was satisfactory. Shrugging her shoulders, she went outside to locate the author of the note.

All the tables were full either with families or cocktail-sipping adults; none of them looked like they were expecting her. She realised that third on the right was set a little way back from the edge of the pool and shielded from view by a large plant with wide green fronds so she couldn't make out who was waiting for her. When she saw the jug of dark maroon liquid on the table, she knew immediately who had left the note.

'Amir,' she said, and was answered by a wide smile of welcome.

'How did you find out where I was staying? I'm so glad you did. I wondered if I would see you again. Did you get into trouble? The Chief of Police seemed to know who you were.'

'Enough questions,' he laughed. 'I asked the bell boy at the Orient. I told him I had to return an item of yours and he found out for me.'

'That was clever,' said Lottie.

'And yes, I did get told off. But don't worry, the General is a pussy cat if handled properly.'

Lottie wondered how on earth the Chief of Police could be a pussy cat, but didn't press the point.

'Where were you this morning?'

'We went to Count Zindani's for lunch.'

At the mention of the Count, Amir's brow furrowed.

'Be careful of him. He's not as pleasant as he makes out.'

'I thought so too,' said Lottie. 'He has so many treasures, and I found a secret room with maps of archaeological digs and a list of buyers and the type of artefact they want.'

'I'm not sure if it's legal to sell those things, but even if it is, he's not to be trusted.'

'I also found a letter from Dr Baramki at the University saying items from my father's dig have gone missing.'

'Did you tell your Aunt?'

'Gosh no. She and him were as thick as thieves. She wouldn't believe me anyway.'

'Have you heard from your father?'

'No, and no one's telling me anything. I'm worried about him. He never misses the summer holidays.'

Amir poured the *jalap* and they continued chatting. A couple of tables away, a blonde-haired, portly man, in a cream linen suit was holding up a newspaper and looking in their direction. He caught Lottie's eye and immediately ducked down behind the pages. Lottie watched him mopping his brow with a red spotted handkerchief, the heat clearly too much for him. She nudged Amir.

'Don't look round, but I think the chap over there in the cream suit is watching us.'

Amir stood up and stretched and fiddled with the umbrella so that he could look. He caught the man peering over the top of his newspaper then immediately disappear behind it when he realised Amir was looking.

'I see what you mean. Let's go for a swim, maybe we can take a closer look.'

Slipping off their tee shirts and shorts, they raced to the pool and jumped in. They splashed about noisily, spraying each other extravagantly near the man's table, forcing him to retreat from the edge of the pool.

'That'll show him,' laughed Lottie.

They had a lovely half hour in the pool, and then Aunt Helen appeared.

'Charlotte, we have to go out. I want you upstairs and ready to leave in fifteen minutes.'

'Can't I stay here? You said six o'clock.'

'No, you may not. Plans have changed. Come along, quick smart.'

Reluctantly, Lottie dragged herself to the edge of the water.

'How will I contact you?' she whispered to Amir as soon as Aunt Helen had moved away

'Hadi, the bell boy. Give him a note. He will know where to find me. I'll stay in the water a little longer so your Aunt doesn't notice me.'

But he was too late. Aunt Helen was already aware of the local boy talking to her niece. *I shall be keeping a very close eye on you,* she thought.

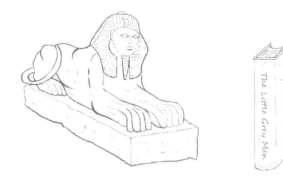

Going to Byblos

Fifteen minutes later, Lottie was showered, dressed and sitting in a taxi with Aunt Helen.

'Where are we going?'

'To Byblos. It's the town where your father was… is working. I thought we could visit the site and check his hotel in case they have heard from him.'

'You think something's happened to him, don't you?'

'No Charlotte, I do not. He's obviously following a lead for a new discovery and, typical of your father, has omitted to tell anyone. He was always doing it when he was young. There would be a rumour of a discovery halfway around the world and he would be off.'

'Didn't he ever tell you where he was?'

'Only when his money ran out, then we would get a telegram. It drove your grandparents mad with worry. He was always so impetuous and irresponsible.'

'But he's older now, with a proper job and well... with me.'

'A leopard never changes its spots, Charlotte. You would do well to remember that.'

Lottie couldn't imagine her Papa running off somewhere without telling her. Despite what she said, looking at her Aunt's face, she thought she detected a slight furrow in her brow.

An hour and a half later they arrived in Byblos and the taxi dropped them outside a modest hotel that looked more like a family home than a business. A plump lady in her sixties, with jet black hair tucked untidily under a scarf, came out to meet them. Her face bore the creases of one who has spent too long in the sun. Her eyes smiled when she greeted them, and Lottie liked her immediately. The owner, as she turned out to be, was a little wary of Aunt Helen at first, but when they explained that Lottie was the Professor's daughter, she smiled delightedly and came and squeezed Lottie tightly.

'Marhaba. Welcome, welcome.'

Aunt Helen nodded towards the rooms. The old lady took a key from a board behind the desk and led them up three flights of stairs to the topmost room in the hotel and let them in. Lottie knew straight away why her father had chosen this room.

The large, airy space had two windows, one facing the sea and the other with a clear view of the castle. He had moved the table under the window facing the castle, and she pictured him sitting there writing up his notes after each days' excavation. The table had notebooks and reference books piled on it next to a wooden pen holder with the word 'Byblos' embossed down the centre. Aunt Helen opened the wardrobe, which still had half a dozen shirts and a couple of pairs of trousers hanging inside.

While Aunt Helen went through the pockets and the notebooks, Lottie flopped onto the bed, and noticed a book on the bedside table: *The Little Grey Men* by BB, and next to it his miniature of the great sphinx at Giza lying on its side. Lottie knew immediately what that meant. Her father was in trouble. It was their secret signal at home. If visitors came that he didn't want to see or if he needed rescuing from some dreary parish council meeting he'd been forced to attend he would leave the sphinx on its side. That was her signal to either turn the visitors away or make up an urgent reason for him to come home.

Once, when Mrs Ponsonby, the head of the parish council, tried to press gang him into joining one of her various committees, Lottie had covered her hands and face in tomato sauce and run screaming into the sitting room crying that she had just fallen out of a tree. Horrified at so much blood, Mrs Ponsonby had exited in a flash.

'I've never seen her move so fast,' laughed the Professor later. 'And genius use of the ketchup. I shall have to enrol you into drama school.'

This time though, Lottie knew it meant that her father was in real trouble and needed her help. The book too, was important. It was their favourite, and the one they always used when sending clues to each other. She thought about telling Aunt Helen, but then she remembered how closely she had spoken to Count Zindani and decided not to. Instead she picked up the book.

'What's that you've got there?' asked Aunt Helen, sharply.

'It's a book Papa likes to read to me. I guess he was going to bring it home. It's all right if I take it, isn't it?'

'Yes, yes a story book is of no importance.'

That's where you're wrong, thought Lottie.

'You have something else in your hand. Show me.'

Reluctantly, Lottie opened her hand to reveal the sphinx. Aunt Helen frowned when she saw it.

'It was by his bed. Please may I keep it? It's the sphinx at Giza.'

'I am well aware of what it is and what it signifies, thank you.'

'You are?' said Lottie holding her breath.

'Yes. It is a very important ancient monument. Your father and I always planned to go there together.'

Lottie exhaled.

'Everything appears to be in order here. Come along, Charlotte. Next stop is the excavation site.'

They locked the room and handed the key back to the owner. Aunt Helen gave her the number of their hotel in Beirut and asked her to call straight away if she heard anything from the professor.

The excavation site was on the outskirts of town. The area was cordoned off with thin strips of wire too flimsy to keep people away. Two hot and bothered security guards patrolled the perimeter. There was no other activity. All work on the dig had stopped. Lottie strolled around the boundary while Aunt Helen questioned one of the guards.

'No one has been working here for three weeks,' she said to Lottie. 'The students have left, and these gentlemen have not seen your father.'

'Something's wrong, Aunt Helen. Do you think he's had an accident or been kidnapped?'

'I think, Charlotte, that speculation of that sort does no one any good. What I do know, is that my brother must have had a very good reason to leave the excavation. Perhaps he is following up a new lead.'

'That's what you said earlier, but I'm really worried. I just want my Papa.'

'Now, now, Charlotte. It's no good getting emotional, it only addles the brain. Logic and reason are what solve mysteries.'

'So, you admit that something mysterious is going on?'

'What I admit, Charlotte, is that my brother's whereabouts is currently unknown and the Count and I would very much like him to get in touch.'

At the mention of the Count, Lottie knew that she had been right not to tell Aunt Helen about her father's secret message. This was a puzzle she had to solve on her own. But how? She was in a foreign country with no friends. Lottie mulled over this difficulty while they walked back into the heart of the town. A beautiful courtyard was in front of them filled with tables and chairs. The brightly coloured cushions lifted Lottie's mood. Purple, orange, blue, each colour belonged to a different café. The simple wooden tables were neatly arranged under a canopy of bright pink bougainvillea that grew through a net suspended across the courtyard, providing shade for the customers from the hot sun. They chose a table with purple seats and a waiter appeared at their side to take their order, tea for Aunt Helen and lemonade for Lottie.

'Are you hungry? I'm sure you must be.'

'I am a little.'

Aunt Helen ordered them a salad called *tabbouleh*, a dish of hummus and one of baba ghanoush, all served with the local flat bread.

Lottie tucked in ravenously.

'This is delicious. I really love this one,' she said pointing to the baba ghanoush.

'That is made from aubergines,' said Aunt Helen.

'I have no idea what they are,' replied Lottie, 'But I wish we had them in England.'

'Perhaps one day we will.'

Lottie was extremely doubtful about that, but it only made her more determined to enjoy the food while she was in Lebanon.

When they had finished, Aunt Helen took them to the *souk*. The ancient market was situated on a cobbled street. All the shops were built into the medieval castle walls. Lottie wasn't sure what she liked best, the brightly coloured pottery or the gold figurines of ancient Phoenicians and their alphabet.

'Look Aunt Helen, it says that all modern alphabets began with this Phoenician one. Isn't that amazing? No wonder Papa loves working here.'

'Yes dear, I did know that. They had hieroglyphs as well, but no one has found the key to decipher them yet.'

'Maybe Papa will. He's clever enough.'

'Yes he is,' agreed Aunt Helen.

Other shops had fabulous silks or carpets or paintings as well as postcards and keyrings. Lottie bought some cards and keyrings with a cedar tree for herself and Mrs Button. She was trying to stop herself from worrying, but it wasn't really working. The next shop was a fossil museum. Inside the domed building were large fish fossils with detailed histories of where they had been found. There were also fossils for sale with certificates of authenticity. Lottie was very excited by these.

'Aunt Helen, please may I buy one for my friend Diana and one for Papa? I still have some pocket money left.'

Aunt Helen sniffed. 'You may buy one for your friend, but I don't think the Professor would want one. He is an archaeologist, not a palaeontologist.'

Hearing her mention a professor, the shopkeeper approached them.

'I am sorry to intrude, but you mentioned a professor.'

'Yes, my father, Professor Evans. He's working on an archaeological dig near here.'

'Then I have something for you.'

The man opened a drawer behind the counter and took out a small package.

'The professor bought this fossil. He said that it was for his daughter and someone would be in to collect it. That was three weeks ago.'

'Three weeks ago!' said Lottie. 'And you've not seen him since? How did he look?'

'I would say he looked very well. He said he worked for the American University. Such a nice man. Really took time to study the fossils. He was most particular that you had this one. He said you would know why.'

Lottie carefully unwrapped the packet. Inside was a small fish fossil called an armigutus, perfectly preserved in sandstone.

'Wow, it says here that it is one hundred million years old. That is amazing. I wonder why he chose this one though?'

'Yes, it is dear, but it is time we were leaving. Thank you for your help sir. Much obliged.'

Aunt Helen hurried Lottie out of the shop and on towards the car waiting to return them to Beirut. Lottie studied the fossil carefully, turning it over and over in her hand. It really was a beautiful thing. She read its certificate telling her where it was found, what date, its age. There was another series of numbers on the back of the certificate, 53,28,3, 4. Lottie tried to puzzle out their meaning.

'What do you think, Aunt Helen? 53 million years, 28th March 1904., perhaps that's when it was found.'

'Not if it's 100 million years. Perhaps they are just an item code for the museum.'

Code, thought Lottie. *How stupid of me.*

Aunt Helen remained her usual silent self for the rest of the journey. Lottie's anxiety about her father's whereabouts was stronger than ever. *The shopkeeper was expecting this to be collected. Does that mean Papa knew he was going away? Aunt Helen said that he used to just take off to places. Did he know that we would come looking for him? Is this a message or just his way of saying 'don't worry'?* All of these thoughts tumbled round and round in her head. *I wish grown-ups would talk more. When Diana and I are worried about something we discuss it.* Her tummy ached and she realised she was feeling lonely. *I could really use a friend right now,* she thought.

Aunt Helen's Meeting

Aunt Helen left the hotel room early the next morning, her attaché case firmly clasped in her hand. The note she had left for Charlotte had clear instructions that she was to stay within the hotel complex. Aunt Helen seriously doubted that her niece would do as she was asked, but she had taken steps to prevent her from disobeying.

A dark saloon car pulled up outside the hotel and Aunt Helen got in and it sped away. The driver said nothing to her, he merely nodded an acknowledgement of her presence. The Beirut traffic was its usual chaotic self: cars pulling out in front of each other, horns blaring. It occurred to Aunt Helen that there were remarkably few collisions considering the nature of this mad highway dance.

The car took her downtown to the business district, pulling up outside a four-storey building, whose creamy yellow façade blended perfectly with the rest of the street. A series of archways on the ground floor beckoned visitors towards its inner courtyard, where a circular fountain shot upwards in perpetual motion. Small cedar trees, the national symbol of Lebanon, stood guard around the perimeter. Aunt Helen entered through the second archway, crossed the courtyard and ascended a narrow staircase to a first-floor office. Knocking once, she entered.

'Good morning Miss Evans. Please sit. Do you have the information I require?'

Aunt Helen sat down on the proffered chair, barely glancing at the small dark-haired man behind the desk, except to note that he needed a shave. The stubble on his chin made him look unkempt, which irritated Aunt Helen as she thought it slovenly. Sensing her disapproval, the man apologised for his appearance.

'I have been at the docks all night waiting on a shipment.'

'And?'

'Nothing.'

Aunt Helen placed her attaché case on her lap, deftly entering the correct combination to open the locks, then lifted out a sheaf of papers.

'Manniger is expecting a particularly fine Greek marble. I believe that it is ready to go,' she said.

'Yes, my men were tracking it through Syria, unfortunately its current whereabouts is… unknown.'

Aunt Helen frowned, 'And the Persian bronze for the McCall woman?'

'All in hand. We expect to take possession of that when it reaches Paris.'

'Good. Any word on the Byblos tablet? I believe my brother may have interfered in that one.'

'Nothing. Have you managed to locate him?'

'Unfortunately not. I do have people looking, but so far nothing has come to light.'

Aunt Helen handed over the papers.

'These detail the movements of the other shipments, together with the expected storage details for the Manniger marble and who the contacts are. The Count is taking particular precautions with it because of the size. The Persian bronze was much easier for him to ship, as you will see from my notes. The rest of the items are still being sourced. I will contact you again when we have identified their point of origin. I will now go and speak with the Count to ascertain whether he has had any luck locating my brother. Do you have the figurine?'

'Yes.'

He handed over a small statue carefully wrapped to protect it.

'If I can entice the Count to buy them, we will have everything we need to close this chapter. In case the other items don't work for us.'

Aunt Helen placed the figure in her case and snapped it shut, then stood up, indicating that their meeting was over. The small man bowed and opened the door for her. The driver was waiting when she exited the building.

'Count Zindani's villa,' she said, before sitting in the back. Once more the car sped through the Beirut streets and out onto the mountain road that led to Aley. Traffic was lighter on this road and they arrived quickly to find the Count waiting for her.

'My dear Lady, what a pleasure to see you.'

He raised her hand to his lips and kissed it gently. Aunt Helen gave nothing away, looking straight at the Count as she withdrew her hand.

'Any news on your brother?'

'None, which is really rather tiresome. However, I do have movement on that other matter we discussed.'

'Oh, yes. But where are my manners, keeping a lady waiting on my doorstep? Please come in and take tea upstairs, where we can discuss things in more detail.'

'Thank you, Count. That would be most welcome.'

She followed him inside and upstairs to his magnificent sitting room, where a new item immediately caught her attention. It was a large piece of marble depicting several figures feasting.

'From the Hellenistic period, if I am not mistaken,' she said.

'It is. Sadly, I am merely curating it while a museum space is made available.'

Aunt Helen raised an eyebrow.

'I am surprised the museum agreed to part with it.'

'My security is the best, and they felt that it would be safer here away from the work.'

'Yes, I can see the logic in that.'

The butler appeared with the tea and the Count steered her away from the marble towards the window, where two elegant, wing-backed chairs, upholstered in plush red and gold striped velvet, faced outwards, enabling their occupiers to enjoy the panoramic view of Beirut afforded by the window. Aunt Helen took a moment to look out, then sat down and opened her attaché case once more, this time taking out a package. She opened it to reveal a small golden figurine. The Count's eyes lit up when he saw it and he reached out with his long pincer-like fingers to take it from her, turning it over, examining it carefully, testing the weight in his hand. He took a small magnifying glass from his pocket and passed it over the figurine several times until he was satisfied with its authenticity.

'This is a splendid piece. Splendid. How many did you say there are?'

'Currently we have uncovered twelve, but there may be more. Do you think that you will be able to place them?'

The Count gazed steadily at her, weighing up his next words very carefully. Aunt Helen sensed the greed in his eyes.

'That will depend on the price and your discretion. Anything we negotiate must be watertight.'

'I give you my word as an Englishwoman, that the only people who will know are my handlers, and they have too much at stake to be indiscrete.'

'Very well,' said the Count. 'Let's talk terms.'

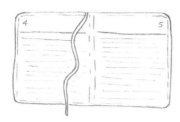

A Visit to the University

Later that morning, Lottie awoke to see the usual instruction to stay in the hotel. Naturally, she had other ideas. She found Hadi the bellboy, and gave him a note for Amir asking him to meet her by the pool at ten o'clock.

While she waited, Lottie swam and collected her thoughts. *Papa has gone somewhere. Aunt Helen and the Count might be working together. The Count has a list of buyers. The sphinx means Papa wants help, but what sort? It's a puzzle, and I'm good at puzzles.* Up and down the pool she swam, trying to think what to do. The water was cool; already the hotel's temperature

111

gauge read thirty degrees centigrade. The day was building into another scorcher.

It was on her third lap that she spotted him. Same cream suit as before, and she could just make out the corner of a red handkerchief in his breast pocket. Once again, he was reading a newspaper, but occasionally he would glance around.

Who are you? And why do I keep seeing you? Whoever he was he made her feel uneasy. Lottie got out of the pool and sat on the side. A waiter was taking orders from guests on the sun loungers. When he walked past her, she jumped up and followed behind him for a few paces, before scampering back into the hotel lobby. The man in the suit glanced over his paper, realised she was gone and began frantically scanning the pool area for any sign of her.

Lottie observed him from the safety of the hotel. *So you were watching me,* she thought. *I will have to be more careful.* Passing a second note to Hadi, telling Amir to come up to the room, she went upstairs to change and wait for him.

There was a gentle knock on the door and she let a smiling Amir into the room.

'Hello. Why the change of plan?'

She told him about the man in the cream suit.

'I think I saw him pacing up and down the hotel lobby looking very flustered.'

'That's because I gave him the slip. He didn't see you, did he?'

'No. I was careful. What do you want to do today? We could go to the Wimpy bar or explore Hamra Street.'

'Actually, I need your help.'

Lottie explained her father's secret signal and the fossil, and how no one had seen him for three weeks, but all his things were still in his hotel.

'He left that message so I would know that he was in trouble.'

'How are you going to find him?'

'He will have left clues. I think this fossil might be one. See these numbers on the back of the certificate? I'm sure they are a code; I just haven't figured it out yet.'

Amir thought for a moment. 'Why don't we try his office at the University? I'll take you. It's not far from here.'

'Yes. Perfect. Will they let us in though? I mean, they'll know we are not students. We're not old enough.'

'Don't worry about that. If anyone asks, we'll say… well, we'll say the truth. That your father works there, and that we've come to meet him.'

Lottie grabbed her notebook and sunglasses and then at the last moment, picked up the copy of *The Little Grey Men* her father had left and popped it into her shoulder bag. They took the fire escape rather than the lifts so they could avoid the lobby and the man in the cream suit. Once outside, Amir led them quickly through a maze of streets, finding his way easily.

After about ten minutes they turned into a wide road with a mixture of shops and restaurants on one side and a long wall overhung with trees draped in jasmine and bougainvillea, on the other.

'This is it,' said Amir proudly. 'The American University of Beirut. The entrance is just down here.'

The two of them slipped past the security guards unnoticed. They went down some steps and headed left up a wide tree-lined avenue with department buildings on either side. Through a gap in the trees, Lottie saw the sea glinting in the morning sun.

'How will we know where Papa's office is?'

'Easy, we just find the archaeology department. All the buildings have their department names on display, and look – there are signposts too.'

They soon located the department and its museum. Due to the summer vacation there were few people about and they were able to enter the building unseen. Inside was a labyrinth of corridors, and they had to guess which ones to go down. Luck was with them and they quickly found her father's office. The door boasted a gold plaque saying

Professor C. Evans. Visiting, in black letters.

Amir tried the handle.

'Locked.'

'Can you give me a leg up?' asked Lottie.

'A what?'

'You know, lock your fingers together to make a stirrup with your hands for me to stand on.'

Looking somewhat puzzled, Amir did as she asked. Lottie put her foot onto his hands and he hoisted her up in the air until she could reach the top of the doorframe where her fingers felt along the ledge.

'Bingo.'

She jumped down triumphantly holding the key.

'How did you know to look there?'

'Papa leaves his study key there at home. He doesn't often lock it, only when Aunt Helen or some other ghastly relative is visiting. Let's get inside before someone spots us.'

Lottie could tell that her father spent very little time in there. It was far too tidy. The shelves housed reference books and journals all lined up neatly and there was a pile of essays on the floor waiting to be marked. Lottie smiled, remembering how he always left his 'homework', as he called it, until the last possible moment. There was nothing

117

significant on the desk, a pot of pens, a filing tray of letters, a large desk diary and a photograph of Lottie and her mother.

'She is very beautiful,' said Amir, looking over Lottie's shoulder. 'Your mother?'

'Yes, she was. She died nearly five years ago. Leukaemia.'

'Oh, I'm sorry, you must miss her'

'Terribly. Everything changed when she died. Papa was devastated and spent even more time away from home, isolating himself from everyone. I had to go to boarding school. I hated it at first, being away from home and missing my mum. Mrs Button, our housekeeper was marvellous. She would send me homemade treats, scones and jam, flapjacks. She even sent a massive Victoria sponge for my birthday. I was very, very sad for ages. It helped a lot when Diana started at the school. We became best friends. After a while Papa started writing to me, which was comforting and he always, always came home for the summer holidays, which is why I know something is wrong.'

'That must have been a difficult time.'

'It was, but we managed. What about you? Do you live with your parents?'

'Yes, but they are hardly ever at home. My father is… busy with work and my mother…' he raised his eyebrows. 'My mother thinks only about her looks and her jewellery. She spends all of her time either at the beauty salon or with her friends. I'm not even sure that she remembers I exist. However, that does mean I am free to come and go as I please and that suits me, because it means I can help you without anyone asking awkward questions. Let's see what we can find.'

Amir looked through the letters, while Lottie flicked through the desk diary. Mostly it was lecture times and meetings or dates for the dig at Byblos. The last entry was just over three weeks ago. It was short and consisted of two letters and three numbers. BB 69, 10, 6. Lottie copied it into her notebook.

'Why are you writing that down? It doesn't make any sense.'

'It does to me,' laughed Lottie. It's a code Papa and I use. I knew those numbers on the fossil were significant. Is there anything amongst the letters?'

'Nothing that I can see, except he's written himself a note that just says '*saj.*' He must have been hungry that day.'

Voices in the corridor silenced them. Footsteps approached and someone tried the door handle. Luckily Lottie had had the foresight to lock it from the inside. Whoever it was went back down the corridor. Lottie exhaled deeply.

'They'll be back. Time to leave.'

Cautiously opening the door, Amir peered out.

'All clear,' he whispered.

Lottie followed him, making sure to relock the door, before running swiftly to the exit. They ran towards a grassy terrace and sat down. Pulling out the copy of *The Little Grey Men*, Lottie showed Amir how the code worked.

'It's a game we played at home. We would leave messages around the house. The numbers are the page, the line and the word. Look.'

'Why this book?'

Because it's our favourite and it's set in Warwickshire where we live. We both have a copy. This is Papa's. He left it with the sphinx. I should have realised then that he would use this code. I'm such a dullard.'

'A what?'

'It means I'm stupid. Too slow.'

'You're not stupid and you've worked it out now. What do the first two clues say?'

Lottie turned to page 53.

'The first clue says *lay low*. But from who? And the second one is *up*.'

'Count Zindani would be my guess,' said Amir. 'The question is why?'

Lottie thought for a moment. 'Do you remember that letter I found from Dr Baramki about the missing artefacts? Maybe Papa realised the Count was stealing them.'

'Yes. And the Count threatened him, so he had to go into hiding.'

'No. If Papa had been threatened, he would have gone to the authorities. He's more likely to be hiding the treasures to stop the Count from finding them. We have to track down the remaining clues. I think I know where we can find another one. Are you hungry?'

Amir looked puzzled for a moment, then grinned.

'I'm sure I could manage a *saj*.'

The Burger Bar

The opposite side of the road to the university was lined with shops, stationers, cafés and at least three *saj* sellers.

'Students are always hungry I think,' said Amir.

'How do we know which one?' said Lottie.

'I guess we just ask them if they know your father. If he has left a message with one of them it will be someone he visits regularly.'

They approached the first shop, but he said that all of his customers were students. The second one was the same, but when they got to the third, the owner knew immediately who they meant.

'Yes, yes, the English professor. Very fine gentleman. Very fine. And you are his daughter? How marvellous. No, I haven't seen him for a few weeks now. I thought he must have gone back to England because when he is on campus, he eats here every day. He says that I serve the finest *saj* in the whole of Lebanon,' said the man proudly. 'You must try. Here is my menu.'

There was so much to choose from. Lottie thought back to her first taste of these rolled up hot sandwiches.

'What does my father like?' asked Lottie.

'Oh yes, he said if his family came here, I was to give them his three favourite ingredients.'

'Three?' said Lottie, looking at Amir.

'Yes, three in particular, I remember now. *Zaatar, which is dried sage, jibne, a hard cheese* and *zaytoon-olives.*'

Lottie scanned the list of ingredients. 'Look,' she said to Amir. '32, 3, 6. That must be the next clue. I'll write them in my notebook.'

To the man she said, 'That sounds lovely, thank you. We'll have two of those. Did my father ever tell you about his work?'

The man shrugged, 'Not in detail, Miss, but I can tell you that he was very excited about a discovery he had made, an artefact that was going to be a major breakthrough in Phoenician history. Did you know that we are descended from the Phoenicians?'

Lottie was suddenly aware of two heavy-set men standing outside the next shop who appeared to be listening intently to their conversation. Nudging Amir, she inclined her head in the direction of the men. As soon as their sandwiches were ready, they took them and with a promise to return, set off up the road at a fast pace. The two men followed.

'Who do you think they are?' whispered Lottie.

'I don't know, but they don't look friendly.'

Making sure that they kept to very busy roads, Amir took them back up to Hamra Street. They saw a group of children playing on a piece of derelict land and mingled with them, eating their food and watching out for the men. At first, they thought they had lost them, but then they appeared at the end of the street, pretending to have a conversation. Amir spoke to the other children in Arabic, pointing out the men on the street corner. The oldest boy nodded and then at a signal from him, the children ran up to the two men asking for money, surrounding them and keeping them distracted while Amir and Lottie dashed off in the opposite direction.

The children crowded around the two men until the oldest boy was sure Amir and Lottie had got away. One of the men handed out a five dollar note and the children ran away to share out the spoils. With their quarry out of sight the men shouted angrily.

Amir and Lottie wandered along Hamra Street, calmer now that their pursuers were gone. This was a mistake; it wasn't long before the men found them outside a kiosk buying sweets. If Amir hadn't dropped his change and bent down to pick it up, he would not have noticed the men lurking outside a nearby café. He nudged Lottie, who realised they had been seen again.

Walking quickly, Amir steered her into the Four Steps Down bookshop where they browsed history books and adventure stories, hiding behind the book stacks as the two men entered the store. The first man spoke to his associate and Lottie noticed the glint of a gold tooth as he sneered at a customer who accidentally brushed against him. She was glad they had managed to conceal themselves behind a bookshelf. Fortunately, the bookshop was huge and there were plenty of aisles for the children to weave in and out of as they avoided their pursuers.

'What are we going to do? We can't stay here all day,' said Lottie.

Amir peered cautiously around the end of the aisle.

'We'll make a run for it., he said quickly. 'Are you ready?'

Lottie nodded.

'Upstairs, turn left, we'll go to café Al Hambra. It's about a hundred yards down the road on the left.'

He grabbed her hand and they sprinted for the entrance while the two men were heading down an aisle towards the back of the shop. They would have made it, except Lottie collided with a shop assistant struggling with a pile of books, which he dropped with a loud clatter.

'I'm so sorry. Let me help,' said Lottie, her innate politeness overriding the need to run.

'No time,' said Amir, and pulled her on just as the two goons appeared at the end of an aisle and spotted them. Lottie and Amir disappeared from view into the crowded street, reaching the relative safety of the café. The Al Hambra was attached to the cinema. Amir bought them tickets for the James Bond movie, Thunderball, which had a special showing that afternoon. The screen was packed with cinema goers who had missed seeing it on its first release and American tourists who were just glad to see something familiar.

'They won't bother us in here,' said Amir. 'Too many people, so we may as well enjoy the movie.'

Lottie kept one eye on the entrance doors at the bottom of the steps. Several more people filtered in before the start of the film, but the two thugs were not among them. The movie was exciting, but watching Sean Connery being chased by large, ugly baddies made her feel decidedly uncomfortable. It was only towards the end of the film that she finally relaxed. When the credits began to roll, they stood up to leave, taking care to position themselves right in the centre of the exiting crowd. Once outside, Lottie scanned the street for the two men. There was no sign of them, but in the throng of people she did notice a man in a cream suit moving off to the left.

'It's the man from the hotel. I'm sure of it. Look, cream suit.'

'Lots of tourists wear cream,' said Amir. 'And even if it is him there's no way he would have known we were here. He probably just wanted to see the film. James Bond is very popular. Maybe he imagines he could be a spy,' he laughed.

Lottie's nerves were too on edge to find this funny.

'I know what will make you feel better. Let's try the new American restaurant, The Wimpy Bar. It's very good.'

The Wimpy Bar was bright orange and white, and Lottie looked round excitedly. She saw flashing neon signs inviting you in to a mix of purple and orange seating. A large counter at the far end was where you placed your order with friendly, English speaking staff in orange and white striped jackets.

'Two burgers and fries please and two cokes,' said Lottie.

'I've wanted to go to one of these for ages. Papa promised to take me, but we never managed it.'

The burgers were as delicious as Lottie hoped they would be. The melting cheese perfectly matched the juicy beef patty. Even the little green pickle had a marvellous tang. She wolfed hers down quickly, the adrenalin of their pursuit had made her hungrier than she had realised. When the food was finished and they were sipping their drinks, Lottie looked up the next clue.

'The next word is *cave*. Does that mean he's found a cave or is he hiding in one?' We still need more information.'

'There aren't any caves in Beirut, but there must be some in the mountains,' said Amir.

'Even if there are, how will we find the right one?'

'Your father must have left more clues. Can you think of anywhere else he might have visited regularly? Did he write to you about a particular place?'

'I don't think so. Maybe we should take another look in…' Lottie gripped Amir's arm. Sitting at a corner table, trying to eat a burger without dropping cheese or tomato sauce down himself, was the man in the cream suit. The expression on his face suggested that he was not enjoying the ordeal.

'Why does he keep appearing wherever I go?'

'He probably just wanted to try a burger. Lots of people do,' said Amir, but even he was beginning to worry.

'Do you think we should tell the police?'

'What can we tell them? I mean, he hasn't done anything wrong and he looks pretty harmless.'

Right on cue a dollop of tomato sauce landed squarely in the man's lap and in his haste to clean it, he stood up and knocked his drink over. The lid flew off and cola spread across the table and onto the floor. All eyes in the restaurant turned towards him, only increasing his embarrassment. A member of staff appeared with a mop and cloths to clear up the mess. Lottie and Amir took advantage of the chaos to slip quietly away, before he had time to notice them go.

The Museum

An hour later Aunt Helen returned to the hotel room and found Lottie asleep on her bed. Lying on the floor was her shoulder bag containing her notebook. Very quietly, Aunt Helen bent down and began going through the pages. There were notes on Lebanon, the airport, the safety instructions from the plane, something about the hideous party dress and the taste of *baklava*;

including a side note that said: *Must give some to Aunt Helen, even she can't fail to enjoy it.* She was about to return it having gleaned nothing of importance, when a glance at the last page revealed something of interest. It read:

Papa in trouble. Left sphinx on its side and BB.
Clue: 53, 28, 3,4 – lay low
Clue: 69, 10, 6 – up
Clue: 32, 3, 6 – cave
More clues needed.

Aunt Helen returned the notebook, opened her attaché case and wrote down the clues in her own journal. She also took out a small Phoenician figurine and studied it carefully.

'That looks like one of Papa's finds,' said Lottie.

Surprised at the interruption, Aunt Helen almost dropped the figure. It was only a smart piece of juggling on her part that prevented it from smashing onto the floor.

'Charlotte, do not creep up on someone like that.'

'I wasn't creeping,' said Lottie indignantly. 'Is it one of Papa's?'

'As a matter of fact, it is. Count Zindani gave it to me this afternoon and asked if I could deliver it to the National Museum's collection. I will take it in the morning.'

'May I come?'

'You may. It will be educational for you and a better use of your time than sitting by the pool all day. If, of course, that is what you have been doing.'

'There's not much else to occupy me in the hotel and the pool is fun,' replied Lottie.

Aunt Helen raised a quizzical eyebrow. 'Indeed, perhaps I should buy you some school books to keep you busy. We can't have you getting bored.'

'Oh no. It's quite all right,' said Lottie quickly. 'Sitting by the pool is really good fun. I don't feel bored at all. Although it will be lovely to see a bit more of Beirut tomorrow and I love museums.'

'Good. Tomorrow at ten. Now time for dinner. Come along.'

They took a taxi to the museum the next morning. From the moment she walked through the door, Lottie felt closer to her father. She knew that he had spent time here; it was the sort of place he loved.

'I have to go and speak with the curator. I shall leave you to enjoy the exhibits. Meet me back here in an hour,' said Aunt Helen. 'Oh, and Charlotte, stay out of trouble.'

Relieved to be on her own, Lottie wandered through the museum. She felt totally at home among the Roman statues, Greek marbles, Phoenician and Egyptian jewellery. There was even a model amphitheatre and she imagined being a gladiator facing a lion or tiger. Included in the items was the sarcophagus of Ahiran, King of Byblos in the tenth century BC, a very impressive item, but the exhibit that really enthralled her was the Colossus, an enormous figure carved out of limestone. It towered above her and she had to crane her neck to study the face.

'Wow,' she said out loud.

'Yes, it is very powerful,' said a man dressed smartly in the museum uniform. 'We are very proud of this one. Sorry, allow me to introduce myself. I am Bassam. Please ask me any questions you have. I am here to help.'

'I'm Lottie,' said Lottie smiling at the tall, neat, middle-aged man in front of her. 'This is a wonderful museum.'

'I am so pleased you like it. I'm afraid not all of our young visitors are as keen as you.'

'That's because my father is an archaeologist, so I've grown up surrounded by history.'

'An archaeologist. Does he have a specialist field?'

'Yes. He's working for The American University of Beirut on a dig at Byblos at the moment.'

The attendant's dark eyes lit up.

'Professor Evans. Yes, I know him. How splendid to meet you. Yes, yes, he often comes here. We have had many discussions about his work. He has uncovered some fine items. So, you are his daughter. He hasn't been in for a few weeks and I do miss our conversations. Is he here today?'

'No,' said Lottie. 'He's missing. No one knows where he is.'

Bassam grabbed her arm. 'Missing?'

Lottie nodded.

'Then come with me. I have something for you.'

He walked off towards a door marked:

STAFF ONLY

'Please wait here. I won't be long.'

Lottie waited by a large statue of a Greek god. A group of Americans wandered through reading the exhibit information cards in very loud voices, as if they were the only people in the building. Hovering near the back of the group, she spotted a familiar figure. *This is not coincidence,* she thought, as the man in the cream suit tried and failed to blend in with the American group. Lottie willed Bassam to reappear. She looked up at the gallery and to her horror realised that the two thugs from the previous day were also milling about.

Unsure what to do, but not wanting to move without speaking to Bassam, she weighed up her options. *I'm in a public place. There are plenty of people. They are not going to do anything to make a scene. Stay calm.* But she couldn't and began to panic, pacing rapidly up and down outside the staff door, glancing up at it every few seconds, willing Bassam to reappear. Fortunately, just as the two men began making their way to the staircase, Bassam emerged from the staff room with a postcard in his hand.

He was about to speak when Lottie shook her head and said in a very loud voice, 'Could you take me to the Curator's office please. I need to meet my Aunt Helen.'

Looking slightly puzzled, Bassam led the way. Once she was confident no one could overhear them, Lottie said, 'I'm sorry Bassam, but I think

143

I'm being followed and I didn't want them to hear what you said.'

'That is most unsettling. Can you still see them?'

Lottie looked behind, but there was no sign of cream suit man.

'Not at the moment. Please show me what you have?'

Bassam handed her a postcard of the museum.

'Your father said that if I heard he was missing, I was to give this to a member of his family who may come looking for him. I don't know why. There is no message on it.'

Lottie took the card and turned it over. It was blank except for three tiny numbers in the bottom right hand corner. 60, 9,6.

'Thank you, thank you. This is very helpful.'

Bassam couldn't imagine why, but he was happy to be of use. Leaving Lottie outside the Curator's office, he took his leave and returned to his post at the colossus, where the two large and heavy-set men were waiting for him.

'What did you give the girl?' said Hassan, the first of the Count's thugs.

'It is none of your business,' said Bassam.

'It is our business and you will tell us,' said Khalid, the second henchman, pushing his forehead right up against Bassam's and standing heavily on his foot. 'Or perhaps you would like to accompany us outside.'

Bassam, glancing at the man's tightly balled fist, did not want to accompany these two anywhere.

'It was a postcard of the museum, that's all. It was a particularly good photograph.'

Hassan twisted Bassam's arm behind his back and was about to push him against the wall when the group of American tourists came around the corner to view the colossus. Hassan let go and he and Khalid moved away. Trying not to shake or have a tremor in his voice after his ordeal, Bassam launched into the history of the statue for the tourists.

Tucking the postcard in her bag, Lottie was about to knock on the office door when it opened and Aunt Helen emerged.

'Charlotte. What are you doing here?'

'I came to find you. I'm afraid I'm not feeling very well.'

Aunt Helen looked at her.

'You do look a little pale. Luckily, I have finished here so we can return to the hotel, where an afternoon in bed is called for.'

'I don't think it's that bad,' said Lottie.

'Don't argue with me, Charlotte. If you are unwell, bed rest is what you need. Come along.'

Lottie followed her Aunt outside to a waiting taxi and climbed in, just as the Count's henchmen exited the museum. With a sigh of relief, Lottie gave herself up to Aunt Helen's care.

Scrabble

A large black Mercedes with tinted windows pulled up outside the National Museum. The rear door opened and the two men got in.

'So, Khalid, Hassan. Do you have any news for me?'

Despite their size and nature, the two men shifted uncomfortably in their seats.

'The girl has made friends with a young Lebanese boy. They spend a lot of time together. The Aunt often leaves her alone. She has not contacted her father.'

'Is that all? What was she doing at the museum?'

'She came with her Aunt.'

'Did she speak to anyone?'

'The Aunt went to the Curator's office. The girl looked at the exhibits and spoke to an attendant. I think he gave her a postcard,' said Hassan.

The Count rested his long fingers under his chin and looked menacingly at his passengers.

'You think. You *think* he gave her a postcard. Gentlemen, I don't pay you to think. I pay you to *know*. Why didn't you find out what was on the card? It could have been a message from her father and I want that man found.'

Khalid and Hassan looked even more uncomfortable.

'The attendant we questioned said there was nothing on the card. She went straight to her Aunt. We did not have an opportunity to see for ourselves.'

'Again, gentlemen, I pay you to make opportunities. If you don't, you will find that our relationship is at an end. And I can assure you that you would not want that. Now find me that postcard.'

The car door opened and the two men got out. Seeing the vehicle they had just exited, a young street urchin thought he would try his luck asking for money, but all he got was kicked and shouted at.

'This English girl is causing us too much trouble,' said Khalid. 'I do not appreciate being told off because of a child. She will pay for that.' He kicked at the pavement but mis-timed it and bashed his toe into the concrete.

'She will pay for that too!' he yelled.

They hailed a taxi and headed to the Excelsior.

Aunt Helen was most insistent that Lottie have a lie down.

'I am fine now, really,' protested Lottie.

'Not in my opinion, Charlotte. You looked exceedingly pale when we left that museum. I can't have you getting ill. An afternoon nap will put you right.'

'But I'm not tired.'

'Nonsense. The heat alone is tiring. Come along, lie down.'

Deciding that it was easier to give in than to argue, Lottie lay on her bed. Before too long the gentle whirr of the air-conditioning lulled her to sleep. Aunt Helen, disappointed that the curator had not had a message from her brother, paced up and down, mulling over what he had said. *He did know the professor and they had discussed his work at Byblos. Count Zindani had attended several of their meetings. He had no news of the professors' whereabouts and he had already told the Count the same.* In her annoyance she accidentally stepped on Lottie's bag which was lying on the floor. The flap was open and her notebook was half out. Aunt Helen picked up the bag, pushing the notebook back in, which was when she noticed the postcard. It was unremarkable, a standard tourist souvenir. There was nothing on the back, but, as she slipped it inside, she noticed the three numbers written just under the photograph information. Frowning, she replaced the postcard in the bag and crossed to the telephone and dialled reception.

'I'd like to place a call please. Yes, I have the number, could you connect me?'

After a brief wait, she was put through.

'There are no new leads. The find has significant value. I believe there are buyers lined up. I will keep you informed. Yes, yes, I understand. The

Count has the contact details. As soon as I have more information, I will call you back.'

Lottie, pretending to be asleep, was listening in to her Aunt's mysterious telephone conversation. It sounded like she and the Count were planning to sell off the treasures from her father's dig. *I will have to be extra careful from now on,* thought Lottie. *How can she do that? Papa always said that she was interested in archaeology too. Now I know why. She's after the money. Oh Papa, if only you knew, you would never have let her look after me.* Thoroughly miserable, Lottie stretched and pretended to wake up.

Aunt Helen, seeing that her niece was waking, dialled reception and ordered tea and pastries to be sent to the room. She had barely replaced the receiver when the phone rang again.

'Count Zindani, how lovely to hear from you. Yes, thank you, I would be very happy to join you for dinner. No, I'm afraid Charlotte will not be able to accompany me. She is a little unwell. Seven o'clock is fine. You'll send the car? Thank you. Until this evening.'

'I'm really much better. I could come with you,' said Lottie.

'No, dear. I think it is better if you stay here. Another time, perhaps.'

Lottie's reply was interrupted by room service arriving with their order. Aunt Helen passed Lottie an iced tea, clearly indicating that the discussion was over. Then, to Lottie's surprise, she produced a travel scrabble from her suitcase.

'I thought you might like a little intellectual stimulation,' said Aunt Helen. 'Your father and I used to have competitions. We kept a score tally for the month and the loser had to clean the other's shoes every day for the next month.'

'Who won the most times?'

'Me, of course. Your father might know some long words, but he wasn't very good at the strategy of the game.'

'Is there a strategy?'

'Oh yes. You have to watch the board and aim to put your pieces on the double and triple word scores. And make words with x, z, j and q, to ensure you can use them if you pick them out.'

Lottie smiled 'Aunt Helen, you really are a dark horse. I bet Papa hated losing.'

'Not as much as he hated polishing the shoes,' grinned Aunt Helen.

'I'd better concentrate then,' said Lottie.

They passed a pleasant hour or two playing the game. Aunt Helen won easily, but Lottie still managed a decent score. When the game was over Lottie felt much more relaxed.

'Thank you, Aunt Helen. That was fun.'

'You will have to improve your vocabulary if you are to register a higher score, but yes, it was enjoyable. Now I must get ready for dinner. Shall I order yours now?'

'Oh no, I'm fine thank you. I'll get something after you've gone.'

'Very well, but nothing too extravagant.'

Lottie read her book while Aunt Helen changed into a plain black cocktail dress and black court shoes. The only hint of glamour was a pair of small diamond stud earrings and an application of lipstick.

'You look very nice,' said Lottie, who was itching for her to leave so that she could work out the latest clue. She hadn't dared to look it up while Aunt Helen was still in the room.

'Thank you, Charlotte. Now you will be all right this evening, won't you? I can cancel if you need me.'

'No, no. I am much better now. I think I might write some letters, to Diana and Mrs Button.'

'If you are sure?'

'I am,' said Lottie. 'Go and enjoy yourself.'

As soon as she was alone, Lottie grabbed the postcard and looked up the next clue. The word was 'pool'. *Hmmm. I need Amir.* Dashing off a quick note, Lottie found Hadi just before he finished for the evening.

'Please can you get this to Amir?'

Hadi smiled 'Yes. Miss Lottie, I'll deliver it on my way home.'

'Thank you, Hadi, Amir said you are a good friend.'

The young bell-boy smiled, barely older than she was, he took great pride in making himself useful to this polite English girl, who always spoke to him with respect. Unlike some of the other tourists

157

who looked down on his lowly position on the hotel staff.

Thirty minutes later, she was sat in a busy café on Hamra Street with Amir, going over the clues.

'So far, we have *lay low, up, cave,* and now *pool.* Can you think where he is?' asked Lottie.

Amir studied the words. 'Maybe it's a cave with water. *Lay low* we know means he's keeping out of the way. He's in a mountain cave or up a mountain, but which one? I will see if I can find out about caves near Byblos. Oh no. Now I'm in trouble.'

Amir tried to hide behind the menu card as General Haddad entered the café, but he was too late. The general had seen him and strode over to their table.

'Amir, what have I told you about coming to cafés in the evenings? And I thought I made it clear to you that this young lady was to be left

158

alone after the party incident. I am sorry miss. I will have one of my officers' escort you back to your hotel. You, young man, are coming with me.'

'No, please. It's not his fault. I asked him to meet me,' said Lottie.

'He should have said no,' replied the General, pulling Amir up by the shirt and marching him out of the café.

While Lottie was wondering how the Chief of Police had known how to find them, she caught a glimpse of cream cotton tucked in at a corner table. *You again.* Incensed about Amir being marched away, she stood up to go and confront him, but the arrival of her police escort prevented her and she was taken swiftly back to her hotel.

Greetings from Lebanon

The Stolen Postcard

As soon as she entered the hotel room, Lottie knew that something was wrong. Her eyes scanned the room. Everything was tidy. Aunt Helen's papers were still carefully arranged on the desk, the beds were neat, her copy of *The Little Grey Men* was laying on the bedside table where she had left it. However, she couldn't shake that feeling of intrusion. Nothing was disturbed in the wardrobes. It was only as she flopped back onto

160

the bed that the realisation hit her. Immediately bolt upright, she stared at the book.

'I left you with the cover facing up,' she said out loud. 'Now you've got the back plate upwards.'

Snatching the book, she flicked through the pages. Nothing fell out. Her father's postcard was missing. Just in case, she pulled back the covers and checked under the pillows. Nothing. A sweep under the bed was equally fruitless as she knew that it would be. In a frantic bid to find it she began stripping the covers from Aunt Helen's bed and tipping out the contents of the drawers in the bedside cabinets.

'Charlotte Evans! There better be a good reason for the mess you are creating,' said Aunt Helen, just managing to dodge a notepad that Lottie had tossed behind her.

'Aunt Helen! Yes, yes there is. It's missing and I really have to find it.'

'Find what?'

Lottie realised her mistake. She hadn't mentioned the postcard to her Aunt when they left the museum.

'Find what, Charlotte?'

'Nothing, nothing.'

'It seems to me that you are making an awful mess for nothing.' Aunt Helen stared hard at Lottie, who looked down at her feet.

'A postcard,' she muttered.

'A postcard! All this for a postcard. Is it diamond encrusted? A limited edition?'

Lottie shook her head miserably.

'No. It's a picture of the museum. Only… only…' She didn't want to say that it was from her father so instead she said, 'It reminded me of Papa.'

Aunt Helen, who of course knew the postcard she was talking about, softened a little.

'Well, I think you have established that it isn't here. I suggest that we tidy up the room.'

'But if it's not here then they must have taken it!'

'And who, exactly, are *they*?'

'Whoever was in our room.'

'And how could anyone have been in our room if you have been here all evening?'

Lottie could have kicked herself. Now she would have to explain where she had been.

'I went for a walk. I was bored.'

'You went out on your own? Charlotte, you are in a strange country! You must control this reckless streak of yours. You can't just go wandering off on your own. Anything could have happened to you.'

'But it didn't. I'm fine. And someone has been in here.'

'Was anything else taken?'

'No.'

163

'So, you are telling me that someone has been into our room and made off with a postcard of the museum. Don't you think that is a little far-fetched? And how could you tell if nothing was disturbed except by you?'

'My book was lying the wrong way up.'

'Your book. Your whole assumption that someone has been in here is based on the fact that you can't remember which way up you left your book.'

Lottie nodded, realising how preposterous it sounded, but she knew. She *knew*.

'I think that you are suffering from too much sun and an overactive imagination,' said Aunt Helen. 'Please tidy this mess up.'

Lottie hung her head and did as she was asked. Despite her outward show of annoyance and disbelief, Aunt Helen knew that Charlotte was a truthful child and if she believed that someone had been in their room, then it was probably true. While Lottie tidied the beds, Aunt Helen checked her desk carefully. Everything appeared in order. Her attaché case was where she had left it, tucked behind the desk. The combination lock still showed the same four digits she had left it on. She was pretty sure who had been there, having spotted the Count's men herself at the museum.

Lottie curled up on her bed, feeling extremely miserable. Aunt Helen walked over and, a little awkwardly, patted her on the back.

'Charlotte dear, I am not without understanding. This has been a trying time for you, in a strange country and missing your father. Why don't we go downstairs and order ourselves two very large hot chocolates and a plate of *baklava*?'

Fighting back tears, Lottie sat up.

'Thank you, Aunt Helen. I'd like that.'

Summer School

When Lottie woke up the next morning, Aunt Helen had not left.

'Good morning Charlotte. I have a rather busy day ahead of me and since you are incapable of remaining within the confines of the hotel, I have arranged for you to attend a summer school.'

'No, Aunt Helen! Please. It's the holidays.'

'I am aware of that Charlotte, but we can't have you getting bored. And we certainly can't have you wandering about Beirut unaccompanied. There is an international summer school run by the American University for the children of the staff and foreign diplomats. You will be fully occupied and more importantly, safe. Now come along, get dressed. We have to be there for 10am.'

Lottie muttered something under her breath which Aunt Helen chose to ignore. She was responsible for her niece and summer school would keep her out of harm's way.

At precisely 10am, Lottie found herself standing in a large hall at the university. Aunt Helen had signed her in and escorted her.

'I will collect you at five o'clock. There is plenty to occupy you, lunch is included so you won't be hungry. You may even make some suitable new friends and possibly enjoy yourself.'

167

'Yes, Aunt Helen, I will try.'

'Well, I must leave you. Goodbye dear.'

Lottie looked around. To her surprise there were about thirty other children there of various ages and nationalities, Eleanor, the American Ambassadors daughter with her perfect ringlets and highly polished shoes, was among them. Luckily, she was too busy talking with a group of equally polished girls to notice Lottie. Their American tones could be heard across the room as they admired each other's clothes and hair. Other students mingled in friendship groups. A tall dark-haired boy wearing a cropped white tee shirt and equally cropped shorts was having a heated debate in French with a blonde boy, in what looked to be a naval uniform. Lottie smiled at the all the arm waving that this entailed.

Although it was a school, the atmosphere was relaxed. Various activities were set out. Lottie noticed chessboards where several students were already playing. Easels and paints were positioned in the right-hand corner facing a window that looked out on the sea. Maths and geography text books sat on other tables. A science corner with all kinds of circuitry on it for experimenting with electricity looked promising, but the area that lifted her heart, was the history table covered in various artefacts for the students to identify and draw and research. This was where she would start. She picked up a figurine.

'Reshef, the Phoenician wealth god,' she said to no one in particular.

'Quite right, bravo,' said a man's voice behind her. 'How clever of you to know.'

The man who spoke had a shock of white hair and a white goatee beard. He wasn't much taller than Lottie, and wore a very crumpled jacket and equally crumpled shirt.

'Sorry, very rude. I'm Professor Malik. I run the summer school.'

'Lottie Evans', said Lottie, proffering a hand, which the professor shook firmly. 'My father is an archaeology professor, which is how I know about the figure.'

'Marvellous, marvellous. Welcome, Lottie. It's very informal here. You may choose the activities you would like to do. Although I have noticed that many of our attendees spend most of the day in conversation, which can still expand the mind and our understanding of each other. However, if you will excuse me, I must go and prevent Marco and Roderick coming to blows over which football team is going to win the world cup this weekend. Roderick is convinced England will do it.'

'Perhaps they will,' said Lottie.

The professor snorted and crossed to the two boys.

Lottie turned her attention back to the history table, picking up other figurines and trying to identify them. Someone peered over her shoulder and she was about to ask them to move away when she realised that it was Amir.

'What are you doing here?'

'My father thought it would keep me out of trouble,' he replied.

'Same,' said Lottie. 'Aunt Helen doesn't trust me to be on my own anymore. Did you find out about the caves?'

'Yes, and I think I know where your father might be.'

'Where? Where?' said Lottie, forgetting to keep her voice down so everyone turned to see what the noise was. Eleanor tutted and tossed her ringlets in disgust at the disturbance; a gesture immediately copied by her little circle of acolytes. Lottie just glared at them. The other students returned to their activities once they realised there was nothing to see, and Amir pulled Lottie into a corner.

'There's a grotto about twelve miles north of Beirut that's got a pool in it. It's a fairly new tourist attraction.'

'If it's for tourists, how can he be hiding there?'

'Because there's an upper cave that isn't open yet. Remember one clue was *up*.'

'Maybe he meant *upper*,' said Lottie. 'That would make sense. We have to go, but how will we get there?'

'I have asked a family friend to drive us there.'

'That's brilliant. Are we going now?'

'No, Friday. We need to stay here and behave ourselves for a few days. We don't want your Aunt Helen locking you in the hotel. If she thinks you are settled in summer school, she won't watch you so closely.'

Lottie, fought her instinct to act immediately, realising that Amir was right. She needed to behave herself. It was her first day and Aunt Helen had probably told Professor Malik to make sure she stayed put.

'Okay, Friday. I'll ask Reza to get us some supplies from the kitchen, I can pick them up on Friday morning. Look out, incoming.'

Amir saw Professor Malik heading towards them and moved away.

'Professor, this history table is fascinating. My father has told me a little of the Phoenicians, but not in nearly enough detail.'

'Well, Lebanon is certainly the place. We have been influenced by many cultures. It was the Greeks who called the people here Phoenicians because of the purple dye that they sold. They were successful traders, you know, but their greatest contribution was undoubtedly their alphabet.'

'Yes,' said Lottie. 'I read about it when I went to Byblos.'

Lottie continued talking to the professor for a while, telling him how much she was enjoying herself and how interesting the history of Lebanon was.

'I think I would like to do some painting now,' she said.

'Certainly, my dear. There is an easel free over there. It was very good talking with you. I will leave you to concentrate on your canvas.' With a small bow he left Lottie to take up a position at the spare easel, where she remained for the rest of the morning, totally absorbed in trying to recreate the view of the dazzling blue sea, in watercolours.

After lunch she played chess with Fritz, a German boy from Hanover, and worked on an electric circuit at the science table with a French girl called Amelie, whose father taught languages. She kept herself busy and avoided Amir so that the professor was able to report truthfully to Aunt Helen that Lottie had made a real effort to fit in.

'I'm very glad your day went well, dear. I'm sure it is much better than sitting around by yourself.'

'Thank you, Aunt Helen. It was quite enjoyable. I beat this German boy, Fritz, at chess, which was very satisfying because he and Roderick have been arguing all day about the world cup. Fritz says England have no chance. If we can't win at football, at least we won at chess.'

'Very patriotic, my dear.'

'May I go for a swim before dinner, Aunt Helen? It is so hot, and I really do love the pool.'

'I think that would be acceptable. In fact, I think I will join you at the poolside and enjoy an iced tea in the sunshine.'

For the next two days Lottie went to school without objection. She was still annoyed about having to go, but now she had something to focus on. Friday would take her to her father, and it was important that she avert attention away from herself. Her assumption that the professor was reporting back to Aunt Helen had been correct. At the end of each day, he and her aunt had a very detailed conversation about all the activities she had partaken of and to whom she had spoken.

Every day, Lottie kept very quiet and occupied herself with activities that required the least supervision. She painted all morning and studied history all afternoon. On her third day she studied the maps of the area in the geography and geology room that had been set up in an adjoining classroom. A post-graduate student had been asked to run slide shows of rock formations and mountain ranges, and she handed round mineral samples for the children to examine. Knowing that her father was probably hiding in the mountains, Lottie paid particular attention to the slides. She learnt that Mount Lebanon is the highest and always snow covered and the highest peak, Qurnat as-Sawda rises 3088 metres above the sea and is higher than Mount Olympus in Greece. *I hope Papa isn't too far up the mountains, we'll never find him,* she thought. The mountains are known for the cedar trees that grow all over them. *That will help him hide,* she smiled.

Amir had not reappeared since the first day, but Lottie wasn't worried. He had said that he would sort out a car to take them to the caves and she had no reason to doubt him. It was better if they weren't seen together, even if she did miss his company. Eleanor and the ringlet gang, as she called them, didn't talk to her. They merely spent their days preening each other and making overexaggerated noises about how marvellous their outfits were. Eleanor loved tossing her head so that her ringlets shook. This became particularly vigorous when Roderick walked past, but he was oblivious to her, his mind totally engaged with football and the upcoming final against West Germany. He and Fritz were continuously arguing. Eleanor saw this as an opportunity to ally herself with Roderick and get him to notice her, standing beside him and nodding affectedly. This was for two reasons; to show off her ringlets and to show her support for England.

'It is fact that the German players are technically more masterful than the English,' said Fritz.

'That may be so,' replied Roderick, 'But the English have more flair. Bobby Charlton is a wizard with the ball.'

'Ha, you will need more than wizardry to overcome the German discipline.'

'Well, I think the English will definitely win,' announced Eleanor, smiling at Roderick.

'And what would you know about it?' scoffed Fritz. 'You are just a girl and an American one.'

'I don't see what that's got to do with anything. I may be an American and a girl but I am still entitled to an opinion.'

'Not about football. They don't even play it in America. We have Beckenbauer, the master technician in our team.'

Roderick snorted. 'We have Geoff Hurst and Alan Ball. We will wipe the floor with you.'

Lottie watched on with increasing amusement. The altercation became so heated that the boys came to blows. Eleanor got knocked over, which elicited a peal of laughter from Lottie as little Miss Perfect was completely dishevelled. Fritz had to go home early with a bloody nose. Roderick was in disgrace, but he said it was totally worth it because

Bobby Moore was definitely going to be the winning captain.

The ringlet gang gathered around Eleanor, making sympathetic sounds and casting ugly stares in Lottie's direction.

'How dare she laugh. How dare she!' fumed Eleanor. 'Ladies, we need to pay her back.'

'Yes, definitely, Eleanor.'

'Marvellous idea, Eleanor.'

'What shall we do?'

'Don't worry ladies, I will come up with a plan.'

'Oh Eleanor, you're so clever. And pretty.'

Lottie guessed they were talking about her, but she didn't care. Seeing the stuck-up Eleanor flat on her back had been so satisfying, even if she did feel a little ashamed for laughing so loudly. She would have loved to have had Diana there to talk to about the afternoons' events. Despite a feeling of loneliness, Lottie thought it was better not to make friends. *If no one talks to me then no one will notice if I'm not here on Friday,* she thought. *The quiet ones are always overlooked. I'll blend in and keep busy, then the Professor won't bother me either.*

In fact, she became so good at busying herself that the Professor completely forgot about her. The constant bickering of the boys annoyed him and the ringlet gang's refusal to partake of any activities was extremely frustrating to him. If he had realised what they were plotting he would gladly have asked them to leave. *Why can't they be more like the English girl?* he thought. She was a model student so he ceased watching her, relieved that at least he didn't have to coax her into behaving.

Lottie tried not to let her impatience get the better of her. Clock watching was not going to make the days pass any quicker. Nonetheless, she had hoped to hear something from Amir. It was

Thursday before he made contact. Hadi bumped into her in the hotel foyer as she made her way towards the lifts after a day at school. In the middle of his over the top apology for Aunt Helen's sake, he managed to slip her a note. She knew exactly who it was from and waited impatiently for Aunt Helen to use the bathroom so that she could open it.

Tomorrow

10:30

Fire escape door

Eleanor's Revenge

Lottie had a restless night; thoughts of tracking down her father were both exciting and nerve wracking at the same time. *What to take with her? Would she get away? Would he be in the caves?* In the end it was sheer exhaustion that put her to sleep, which meant Aunt Helen had a difficult job waking her.

'Do wake up Charlotte, or you will miss breakfast and you cannot go to school on an empty stomach.'

Lottie grunted and turned over, pulling her pillow over her head to try and blot out the light.

'Charlotte, if you are this tired you may stay in bed tomorrow, but it's Friday and you have summer school to attend.'

The only word that filtered through was Friday.

'Friday', said Lottie. 'Friday!'

Her sleep-deprived brain switched itself on as she remembered what was happening today. The covers were thrown back and she dashed to the bathroom. Fifteen minutes later she was washed, dressed and heading downstairs. The breakfast buffet was busy, which was good, and she was able to take extra rolls and pastries, blending in with those guests who returned for seconds. Only Aunt Helen commented on how many times Lottie went back for more.

'Aren't you being a little greedy, Charlotte?'

'I know, Aunt Helen, but being busy makes me hungry, I thought if I had a bigger breakfast it would help.'

'Well, if you really can't last until lunchtime why don't you wrap some of those pastries up and take them with you? I'm sure the hotel won't mind. We are paying for them after all, and I've only had a boiled egg.'

'That is a good idea. I could share with the other girls. I might take some fruit too.'

Well that was a spot of luck, thought Lottie as she packed her shoulder bag with an assortment of the pastries and fruit. *Fancy Aunt Helen being a penny pincher and wanting to get her money's worth.* After Aunt Helen had read her morning paper and drunk her tea they headed back upstairs, Lottie's bag bulging with food. *Water,* thought Lottie, grabbing a couple of bottles from the buffet before they left.

185

'Don't they provide you with drinks at summer school? I'm sure I am paying for refreshments in the fees.'

'Yes, they do, er… but only at certain times and I get very thirsty in this heat.'

'I see. Do you want me to have a word with the professor and ask him to give you more drinks?'

'No thank you,' said Lottie. 'I don't want any special treatment. These will do nicely.'

'As you wish. I just have to collect some papers from our room, and then we can leave.'

Lottie followed Aunt Helen upstairs and waited whilst she put some files into her attaché case, continuously glancing at her watch and pacing up and down, in a bid to make her aunt hurry up.

'For someone who, a few days ago, was complaining about summer school, you seem awfully keen to get there.'

'I've got a chess match against Fritz. It's a decider,' said Lottie, thinking quickly.

'Decider or not, if you would kindly stop pacing, I could concentrate better and then I will be ready sooner.'

Lottie flopped onto the bed. *Calm down,* she told herself. *You're going to give the game away.* Instead, she tried to picture the caves. *Would there be stalagmites and stalactites? How dark would it be? Very dark and cold* she thought. *Dark.* She jumped up and then began scrabbling under the bed for her suitcase.

'What are you doing Charlotte?'

'I've just remembered something I need to take into school today.'

Aunt Helen shook her head. *I will never understand children. Their minds ping from one thing to another far too quickly. I'm surprised they ever manage to learn anything.*

Lottie felt around the pockets on the inside of her suitcase and located the small torch she had

187

packed at the last minute – just in case there was no electricity in Beirut. She squeezed it into her bag.

'Come along, Charlotte. If you are quite ready? We need to leave.'

'Ready, Aunt Helen,' said Lottie, grabbing a cardigan from the back of the door on the way out.

'It's 35 degrees outside, Charlotte. You won't need that.'

'The air-conditioning makes it chilly.'

Aunt Helen locked the hotel room and stared at Lottie. *Sometimes my niece is a little odd,* she thought. *At least with the summer school I no longer have to worry about her getting into trouble.* They set off at a brisk pace and arrived at precisely ten o'clock. After seeing Lottie safely inside, Aunt Helen left to attend to her own business.

'Good morning Professor,' said Lottie.

'Good morning Charlotte. How are you enjoying summer school?'

'Very much, thank you Professor.'

'Good, good. Well I'll leave you to get on. Have a good morning.'

'Thank you, Professor. I will.'

For the next half an hour Lottie spoke to as many of the children as possible, so that they would remember seeing her there. She chatted with Roderick and Fritz about Sunday's cup final. They were still at loggerheads about who would win, but at least they weren't punching each other anymore. She spoke with Amelie about the science table, and even said a passing hello to the ringlet gang. Of course, they refused to acknowledge her, but she knew they had seen her.

At ten twenty-five she slipped, unnoticed, out of the main classroom, only to bump into one of the postgraduate students who helped the Professor.

He was about to stop her when Lottie clutched at her stomach and said, 'Haman, toilet.'

The student, stood to one side and pointed down the corridor. Lottie nodded and hurried on in the direction he had shown her, only stopping when she was sure that he was gone. The fire escape was back the way she had come and then through a grey door on the right. She headed back but found her way blocked by Eleanor and her little gang.

'And where do you think you are going? Sneaking off without permission?'

'I'm not,' protested Lottie. 'I was looking for a toilet.'

'We can help you with that, can't we girls?'

The giggling gang nodded, crowding round Lottie, preventing her from getting away. With their prey surrounded, the group began to sidle along the corridor like a giant ringleted crab.

'Let me go.'

The girls responded by pinching her arms tightly.

'Ow!'

Eleanor grinned devilishly.

'If you come along willingly, it won't hurt.'

Lottie stuck her tongue out.

'So rude. You see, ladies, this English girl has no manners. Perhaps we should teach her some.'

The gang sniggered conspiratorially and pushed Lottie through the toilet door. Once inside, two of the girls blocked the entrance with the large waste paper bin. One of them produced an out of order sign she had made and stuck it on the door.

'Good thinking, Tamara,' said Eleanor.

Outnumbered five to one, Lottie was not going to give in without a fight. She had encountered bullies at school when she had first started at Broadlands and she knew that showing you were afraid was the worst thing you could do. Feet firmly planted, she glared at Eleanor.

'You are nothing but a stuck-up bully,' she said.

'Time to learn that it's not polite to laugh at me,' said Eleanor. 'Do it, ladies.'

Lottie found her arms held tightly behind her back by Tamara, and then a particularly large girl shoved her into a toilet cubicle. Pushing back against her attackers, heart racing, she tried to stop the inevitable, but they were too strong and her head was shoved into the toilet bowl and held there while the chain was pulled. The reek of stale urine filled her nostrils, only to be washed away by the rush of cold water over her head. Coughing and spluttering and gasping for breath, the sound of malicious laughter rang in her ears.

'Again, again,' chorused the gang and Lottie found herself plunged under water a second time.

Soaking wet and utterly humiliated, Lottie sank down to the floor. Eleanor smiled with triumph.

'I'll tell the Professor what you've done,' said Lottie.

'But I haven't done anything. I came in to use the bathroom and found you lying in a puddle because you slipped. Besides, my father is the American Ambassador. Do you honestly think that anyone would believe that I could do such a thing? Really Charlotte, you are even more stupid than you look.'

Checking her appearance in the mirror, Eleanor exited the bathroom, followed by her accomplices.

Lottie stood up, banging her fists on the cubicle door before drying herself off the best she could. 'I hate you!' she yelled at the mirror, tears of rage streaming down her face. 'I hate you and if I didn't have to go and look for my father, you would be paying for this.'

With a deep breath, composure regained, she ran for the fire escape.

Initially, she couldn't see anyone. Then Amir appeared from behind a tree.

'What happened to you?' he asked.

'Eleanor and the ringlet gang. Don't worry, I'm fine. Let's go.'

'Okay. This way. Quickly, before anyone misses you.'

She followed him across the campus and onto a narrow side street where a car was waiting.

'This is Ali. He will drive us to Jeita.'

'Hello,' said Lottie, 'Sucran, thank you.'

Ali smiled 'Anything for my friend Amir. His father has been very good to me and my family over the years. I am glad to help.'

'Yes, yes, old family friend,' said Amir. 'Please Ali, can we go?'

'Yes, Habibi *my dear*. Do not worry. I will take you and your lovely English friend to the caves. No problem.'

The two sat in the car without looking behind them. If they had done, they would have seen another vehicle start its engine and follow them.

The Caves

The road out of Beirut was busy. Horns were louder than ever as a myriad of road users jostled for position, weaving in and out of lanes in an effort to move just a little faster. Lottie hardly noticed; her mind was completely focused on finding her father.

'Do you think Papa will really be in the caves?'

'I do. We will have to get past any workers or security to get into the upper grotto, but we'll find a way.'

It was an eleven-mile drive north of Beirut to the valley of Nahr El Kalb, where the grotto was located. The spectacular scenery of the mountains was lost on Lottie. They could just as easily have been driving through a tunnel for all the notice she took. Ali was talking but she wasn't really listening.

'The grotto was discovered in 1836 by an American, would you believe. It is so beautiful; many tourists go there, but only the lower cave. The upper grotto is being prepared and when it is finished it will be one of the greatest wonders to behold. People will come from all over the world just to see it.'

'I'm sure it's marvellous,' said Lottie. 'How much longer till we're there?'

'I believe we have arrived,' said Ali as they drove past a small sign saying *Jeita Grotto*.

He turned the car into a rough road running along the side of a tall, tree-covered mountain. A man wearing a green coat and carrying a shoulder purse approached the car.

'It is five dollars per person please to see the wonders of the Grotto. Please follow the signs. You may park your car a little further down.'

'I am only dropping off,' said Ali.

Lottie scrabbled in her purse. Luckily, Aunt Helen had given her emergency money, so she had a ten-dollar bill which she handed over.

'I hope I won't need that for school next week' she said.

'If we find what we are looking for, you won't be going to summer school next week,' said Amir.

Ali drove a little further down and dropped the children by a small wooden hut that served as the souvenir shop.

'I am going to have coffee in that café we passed. I will be back in two hours.'

'Thank you,' said Amir.

Before they had chance to move on, a guide appeared and ushered them down an underground passageway.

'This way please, for the marvels of Jeita.'

The sound of rushing water was everywhere. After a few hundred yards the path opened onto a wondrous cave.

'Oh my,' said Lottie as her eyes took in the vast expanse of shimmering pale green water meandering into the heart of the mountain.

'Look at those, Amir,' said Lottie, pointing to the cave roof studded with stalactites of varying shapes and sizes.

It truly was a marvel to behold. They were led on to a wooden jetty and helped aboard a flat-bottomed boat.

'You will see the wonder of the caves as we travel into the heart of the mountain,' said their guide. 'Please be seated.'

As there were no other visitors, they had their own private tour. Despite the outside temperature being in the thirties, in the cave it was more like sixteen and Lottie was glad she had remembered her cardigan. Once they moved away from the jetty the only sound was the quiet rev of the boat's engine as it propelled them slowly on towards the mountain's heart. Lottie felt like she had entered a magical realm, touching the stalagmites as the boat floated past them. They were damp and cold. Her fingers drifted over the side of the boat and she enjoyed the soft coolness of the water. An eerie stillness filled the cavern and it was like being in an underground cathedral, only this was a cathedral of nature, not man-made.

'The stalactites are mostly composed of calcite, formed when rainwater trickles through the rocks picking up minerals. It can take up to a century for a stalactite to grow just one inch,' said their guide.

'So, you can see that this cave is many thousands of years in the making. The stalagmites too, are formed from the drips. See, stalactites and stalagmites always in pairs or in one long column.'

'It is truly amazing,' said Lottie.

'Please mind your heads,' said the guide, steering them under a low outcrop of rock after which the water opened out into an immense pool. Their guide turned off the boat's engine and let them sit there for ten minutes to soak up the atmosphere. Lottie was entranced. The sheer enormity of the cavern, the silence and its other-worldliness enthralled her. For the first time that summer she felt really peaceful, all worries forgotten.

'Magical. I never thought I would be inside a mountain. It's glorious. I wish I could stay here forever. Wow! You are so lucky to work here and see this beautiful place every day,' said Lottie.

'Thank you. Yes, it is beautiful but I'm afraid that this is as far as we can go, although the cave continues for a long distance.'

'Must we go back?' said Lottie.

'I am afraid so,' answered the guide. 'See, another boat is coming through.'

He restarted the engine. A second boat passed the rock and came into the lagoon. This one carried a group of tourists whose loud voices echoed through the cave, shattering the stillness. *Why can't they be quiet and appreciate the beauty?* thought Lottie. Once they had returned under the rocky outcrop, the voices faded and the silence of the cave enfolded them again. The boat chugged quietly back. Lottie drank in the wonders of the mountain, savouring every moment.

'Thank you so much,' said Lottie to their guide when they reached the jetty. 'I will tell all my friends about this place.'

'Sucran, thank you,' said the guide.

'Wasn't that amazing. Wow!'

Amir nodded.

'Are you all right? You look awfully pale.'

'I… I… I need to be outside,' replied Amir. 'Sorry. Can't breathe.'

He rushed on ahead and burst out into daylight with huge relief.

'What happened?' asked Lottie, racing after him.

'I … I guess I don't like being underground. Even though it was awesome, I just wanted to get out of there.'

'I thought you were quiet, but I just figured you were over-awed by the place. You should have told me.'

'You were so happy. I didn't want to spoil it for you.'

'But we have to go into the upper cave to find my father. How are you going to manage that?'

'I'll be fine. Probably just the water.'

He didn't sound totally convinced though.

They carried on up the path until they came to a barrier with a sign saying *Do Not Pass.*

'This is it, come on,' said Amir. There were no staff about, so they crept past the barrier unseen and moved further up the mountainside. Ahead was the entrance to the next cave. Ropes and boots and tool boxes lay abandoned to the left of the entrance.

'Why is no one here?' asked Lottie.

'Friday,' said Amir. 'Day of prayer. That's why I waited until today to come here. I hoped that it might be a day off for the workers.'

'Good thinking, but there may be a security guard.'

Picking their way carefully, the two of them followed the path down into the cave. If the bottom grotto was wondrous, this top one was even more so. An immense cavern lay before them. Stalactites the size of skyscrapers hung down from the ceiling. The floor was pitted and cratered like a lunar landscape. A part constructed walkway led deep into the cavern and was dimly lit by safety lighting, giving the whole place an eerie and other-worldly quality.

'If Papa is hiding in here, he will be much further in,' said Lottie.

Amir nodded, trying to keep his breathing under control. He wasn't a boy given to panic, so he was annoyed with himself at this irrational fear. Lottie took his hand.

'Come on. It's okay. Let me know if you need to go back.'

'No, no. I won't let you down. We have to find your father.'

The rocks jutted out at strange angles and the pathway weaved its way around them. One particular formation looked like giant mushrooms; other stalactites hung down like massive stone curtains. Amir looked up to the roof of this colossal chamber and suddenly felt as insignificant as an ant, which only aggravated his feeling of panic. The walkway ended and they climbed gingerly down onto the cave floor. Lottie took out her torch. The end of the walkway meant the lights finished too.

'I'm glad I remembered to bring this,' she said.

Amir smiled weakly, still struggling to steady his breathing. The floor of the cavern was slipperier than they expected and once or twice Lottie nearly lost her footing, grabbing on to Amir to save herself. Having to concentrate on where to place his feet actually helped to calm Amir a little and enabled him to keep moving.

Lottie felt her way along the cave wall and around an enormous stalagmite the size of a bell tower. She used the torchlight to try and get her bearings. The cave went on and on and on. *How deep does this go?* she wondered. *If Papa is here, how has he survived?* The torch flashed around and this time she noticed a gap in the wall.

'There,' she said to Amir. 'Let's try through that space.'

Amir looked where she was pointing. The pounding in his chest increased, his breath shortened and he knew that squeezing through the narrow crack would not be possible.

'You go. I'll wait here. Call me if you find something.'

His panic was clearly visible. Not wanting to distress him further, Lottie nodded. 'Okay. Shout if you need me. Will you manage in the dark?'

'Yes. Go.'

She slipped through the gap, leaving Amir in almost total darkness. Without Lottie to focus on, his claustrophobia built up again. Faces appeared in the rock; thoughts invaded his mind. *Run! Run before the whole of the mountain crashes down on you.*

'Stop it. Stop it. This place has been here for centuries. It's not going to collapse now,' he said out loud, to try and keep calm.

Try as he might, he couldn't stop the voice in his head urging him to escape before it was too late. To alleviate the panic, he got up and moved around, cursing himself for not bringing a torch. *Maybe there will be one in the toolboxes by the entrance,* he thought. *Yes. Yes. I'll go back and get one.* Very slowly and carefully, he felt his way back along the cave wall, but mountains can be treacherous and he took a wrong turn and found himself stumbling about in the darkness of a side cavern. Something caught his foot and he stumbled forward. He lost contact with the wall and spun around, completely disoriented. Panic engulfed him. His breath came in short pants. *Can't breathe, can't breathe.* Dizzy and frightened, he took a few more steps before the lack of oxygen overwhelmed him. He fell to the floor, sinking into oblivion.

Professor Evans

Lottie pushed through the gap and found herself in a small cavern. She could see signs of human activity: a small pile of carefully placed rocks, marks on the wall that looked like a tally chart and a discarded water bottle. She crossed the chamber and went through a second gap. A larger cavity lay in front of her. There was a rucksack and a water canteen. *It must be the right place,* she thought. The torch cast its light onto a figure huddled into a sleeping bag, who groaned as the light disturbed their slumber.

'Safa, is that you?' said the sleeper.

'Papa, Papa,' yelled Lottie, rushing forward.

Professor Evans sat up and rubbed his eyes.

'Lottie? Lottie is that you?'

'Yes, yes,' she replied, falling into his arms. 'I've been so worried about you. No one knew where you were.'

'Lottie. How did you find me?'

'I followed the clues you left me, of course.'

'My clues, but they were… I should have known that my resourceful daughter would work them out, even in a foreign country. But how did you get up here? Aren't you staying in Beirut? I told Helen to book The Excelsior.'

'Yes, yes, she did. My friend Amir, he helped me with the clues and got us a driver. He knows loads of people; I don't know how. These two men have been following us and I don't like Count Zindani.

Aunt Helen does though, she keeps having dinner with him. And I think he's stealing treasures…'

'Lottie, Lottie, slow down. I take it Aunt Helen doesn't know that you're here.'

'Oh, no I was very careful not to let her know what I was doing. Papa, I hate to tell you, but I think that she is working with the Count. I heard her on the phone to someone about a buyer and I found a list of names in the Count's office of people wanting artefacts.'

'And Aunt Helen hasn't seen any of the clues I left?'

'No. Don't worry. I made sure she didn't see them.'

'I see,' said the Professor. 'So, no one knows that you are here? Good.'

'But now that I've found you, you will come back to Beirut with me?'

'I'm afraid I can't just yet, my darling girl. I'm waiting on a contact from the Embassy. You see I have found something that I believe is the key to deciphering Phoenician hieroglyphs. If it is what I think, it is very, very valuable. You are quite right not to trust the Count. I realised some time ago that various items from the dig were going astray. I told Dr Baramki and we have been working with an international agency to try and gather enough evidence to charge him with illegally selling off ancient treasures.'

'How long will you have to stay here? I miss you so much.'

'I'm not sure. Hopefully not for too long. The artefact is hidden here with me. I'm so sorry I couldn't be home for the summer. I didn't mean to let you down, my darling. You know I hate to put work ahead of you.'

Lottie smiled at her father.

'You haven't let me down. And besides, I've had a wonderful summer so far. I've been on an aeroplane; I'm staying in a hotel with a swimming pool and I've made a new friend and solved a puzzle. I've really had quite an adventure. The hotel is great. It has this machine that keeps the room cool, oh, and I brought you some pastries from the breakfast buffet.'

Professor Evans laughed. 'My dear girl, I have missed you.'

Lottie opened her bag and took out the cakes, passing her father a squished Danish pastry while she had a croissant. They tasted delicious, sharing them in this cave with her father only enhanced their flavour.

'These are really good. I've been living on whatever my friend Safa has managed to leave me. He works with the construction crew. What about your friend, though? Won't he be hungry?'

'Amir! I forgot all about him. The cave makes him feel scared, so he waited in the main chamber.'

'Well, you better get back to him and back to Beirut before you are missed.'

'Are you sure you can't come with us?'

'Not yet my girl, but it won't be for much longer. Once the agency has gathered their evidence I can leave here. At least you know that I am all right, just a little dirty and unshaven.' He squeezed her hand. 'I'll walk you back to the path.'

The Professor lit a small oil lamp and filled the chamber with light. 'This is a little more effective than your torch,' he laughed. 'And I'm guessing, that as you managed to get in here, today must be Friday.'

'Yes, it is,' said Lottie. 'It was Amir who knew to come today.'

'He sounds as resourceful as you. Watch your step. It's this way.'

215

Re-joining the main cavern took only moments,

'Amir,' called Lottie. A shadow crossed the opening. Lottie pushed through expecting to see her friend, but it wasn't Amir who was waiting for them when they emerged through the gap.

'Professor Evans. You have caused us a great deal of trouble,' said Hassan.

'Your daughter too,' added Khalid. 'Only you weren't so clever today, were you? It was only too easy to follow your driver up here.'

Lottie tried to run but found herself lifted clear of the floor.

'Put her down!' yelled the Professor. 'Let her go. I will come with you.'

'You will both come with us. We can't have her running off to the police,' said Hassan.

Lottie continued to punch and kick her captor.

'Tell her to stop or I will stop her myself,' said Khalid.

'Charlotte. Enough,' said the Professor. 'Let my daughter go. She has nothing to do with this.'

'Except she can go blabbing to that Aunty of hers. You are both coming with us. It might make you both more co-operative. We will start by searching in there,' he pointed to the cavern. 'Please lead us, Professor,' said Hassan.

He shoved Lottie and the professor back through the gap. While Khalid stood guard at the entrance, Hassan began kicking over the Professor's things. He shook out the sleeping bag, emptied the rucksack and was about to stamp on a scarf when the professor shouted, 'Don't!'

With a smile, Hassan bent down and picked up the scarf. Unwinding it carefully, he found a fragment of a larger tile.

'Please be careful with that,' said Professor Evans.

'I believe that this is the piece the Count has been waiting for. He has found your deception extremely annoying, Professor. Something, I am sure he will tell you himself when we deliver you to him.'

'You can't just take treasures,' shouted Lottie. 'Or my father.'

'It's all right, my darling. We'll go with these men and sort everything out.'

Lottie wasn't convinced, and held tightly to her father, before Hassan bound their hands behind their backs and led them out of the chamber.

Amir is Caught

Somewhere in the darkness, Amir regained consciousness and sat up. His head hurt and he felt something sticky on his cheek. *Blood*. Gently feeling his face, he found the gash on his forehead from the fall. He sat up very slowly and tried to orientate himself. It didn't matter how wide he opened his eyes or how often he blinked, nothing came in to view. He was in complete darkness, and lost. A noise filtered through to him; it sounded like voices off to his right, so he shuffled slowly towards it. It was difficult feeling his way and he felt the skin on his knees shredding on the rocky floor, but he kept the voices on his right as he gradually made it back to the opening in the chamber wall that he had accidently staggered through. Now the voices were very clear, and he only just managed to duck behind a stalagmite and avoid being seen by Khalid and Hassan, who were dragging Lottie and a man who he assumed must be her father, along behind them.

'Please, a little slower. It's hard to keep steady with our hands tied.'

'We have been slow enough Professor, trying to track you down.'

There was a cry. Lottie had slipped and grazed her knee. Amir quickly covered his mouth to stop himself from calling out to her. But he managed to throw a small pebble at Lottie which hit her on the arm as she stood back up. She spun around to see where it had come from and caught a glimpse of red tee shirt through the gloom, before it disappeared behind the rock. To let Amir know that she had seen him, she said, very loudly;

'My friend will miss me, you know. He will come looking.'

'Ha, if you mean that idiot boy who came up here with you, he has got himself lost in the depths of the grotto. By the time he finds his way out we will be long gone and he will think that you have abandoned him,' sneered Khalid. 'That is, if he actually manages to get out. He might remain lost forever.'

'He is not an idiot,' said Lottie. 'He's smarter than you.'

'Enough,' said Hassan. 'Be quiet and keep moving.'

Once they reached the walkway, the ascent into daylight became much quicker and easier. The professor closed his eyes, the dazzling sunlight too strong for them.

'I can't see. Too bright,' he said, stumbling forward, unable to open his eyes. The sun felt warm on his skin and it was good to breathe fresh air again, but without sunglasses to shield his eyes, he couldn't open them.

'Too long in the dark,' he said to Lottie, sensing her concern.

'Give him your glasses,' said Hassan.

'Why me? Give him yours if you are so concerned,' replied Khalid.

'It is not concern. I just want to move quickly.'

'So, give him your shades.'

'I need them for driving.'

'Well I'll drive.'

The bickering continued until Lottie said, 'I have a pair in my bag.'

The two men turned to her. Hassan tore open her bag and pulled out a pair of bright yellow, star shaped plastic sunglasses which he shoved onto

Professor Evan's face. They were a little small, but they shielded his eyes enough for him to open them a fraction and continue walking the short distance to the car. Lottie and her father were bundled inside and driven off at speed, almost knocking over a tourist coming out of the lower grotto.

Amir, keeping a safe distance, had managed to follow them outside. After allowing a moment or two for his eyes to readjust to the light, he set off down the mountain to find Ali and get back to Beirut. He was running so fast he didn't notice the tourist that the Count's henchmen had narrowly missed. The man stood in the centre of the path, and even though his cream suit stood out from the scenery, Amir didn't see him until it was too late. He was caught in a vice-like grip and was unable to wrestle free. The stern-faced man did not intend to let him get away.

'I think you had better come with me,' he said.

Prisoners

The count's men drove fast, with scant regard for the tight bends or narrow lanes of the mountain road. They had their prize and knew they would be well rewarded.

'I'm sorry I got you involved in all this, Lottie. When I asked Aunt Helen to look after you for the summer, I thought that she would keep you safe.'

'She did try,' said Lottie. 'She even enrolled me into summer school at the university, but I managed to sneak out. Although they have probably realised by now that I'm not there.'

'That's my girl. Always enterprising.'

'Quiet in the back. No talking,' said Hassan.

Lottie snuggled into her father and allowed the comfort of being next to him to wash away her fear about their current predicament. The car sped on and they were soon at the outskirts of Beirut. Instead of heading through the city and out to Aley, the car turned right towards the harbour.

'Where are you taking us?' asked Professor Evans.

'You will know very soon,' said Khalid.

The car pulled up outside a large industrial unit, and the professor and Lottie were hauled roughly out of the back seat.

'This way,' said Hassan, shoving the professor forwards.

The building they entered was a large warehouse filled with wooden crates of varying shapes and sizes. Lottie tried to peer inside one, but all that was visible was the straw used as protective packing. She did notice the name *Manniger* on one of the crates. *Why was that familiar...? The list of buyers in the Count's office!* she thought. Before she could say anything to her father, they had been marched through the warehouse and were descending a metal stairway to a wooden jetty. Moored up, was a truly fabulous yacht. It must have been eighty feet long, with three decks, gold handrails and white leather seats. A table was laid with champagne flutes next to a perfectly chilled bottle of Dom Perignon resting in an ice bucket. The name *Treasure Seeker* was embossed on the side of the boat in large gold letters. Waiting to greet them was Count Zindani.

'Professor Evans, welcome aboard my little boat, and your lovely daughter too. How nice. Do sit down. Khalid, please untie my guests. Perhaps some refreshments?'

'I'm fine, thank you,' said Professor Evans.

'As you wish. You don't mind if I do?'

He clapped twice and the butler appeared and poured him a glass of champagne.

'I must say, that was a fine maze you led us through, Professor. And most inconvenient. I do not appreciate being made a fool of in this way. Where is the artefact that you found?'

Hassan handed over the rucksack. The Count's long fingers felt inside and extracted the tablet. Instinctively, Professor Evans reached out to take it from him and was roughly pushed back into his seat.

The Count, eyes gleaming, lovingly examined the tablet.

'Professor, you believe that this may be the Rosetta Stone of Phoenician hieroglyphics?'

'My early research strongly indicates that it is of great significance, yes,' replied the Professor calmly.

'Indeed. Indeed. If it does prove to be the key to unlocking the hieroglyphs, then this is extremely valuable,' said the Count greedily. 'I have several contacts who would pay handsomely for such a thing.'

'You can't sell it,' shouted Lottie. 'It belongs to the University.'

'It belongs to me, girl,' sneered the Count. 'I will decide who keeps it.'

'I haven't finished authenticating it. I have to try to translate more hieroglyphics,' said Professor Evans. 'There is a lot more work still to be done before it can be confirmed as the key.'

'You do not need to worry about that, Professor. I have a team of experts on standby.'

'You can't!' shouted Lottie again. 'It's my father's work.'

'Take them below,' ordered the Count. 'I grow tired of her whining.'

Hassan yanked Professor Evans to his feet.

'Leave him alone,' said Lottie, pounding Hassan with her fists. Khalid grabbed her, pinning her arms to her side, then lifted her and carried her below decks. The lower levels which housed the engine were plain and gloomy and smelled of oil. Here, away from the glitz and glamour of the upper decks, the Professor and Lottie were tied to chairs, hands behind their backs.

'Not so vocal now, are we?' said Hassan. 'Are you going to stay quiet, or do I need to gag you as well?'

Lottie shook her head.

'Good.'

The men left, slamming the hold door and plunging the prisoners into darkness.

'Lottie, are you okay?'

'Yes Papa. I'm sorry I led them to you. I was trying to help. I thought that we'd been careful.'

'You have helped. I was worried about you, and I'm not sure how much longer I could have stayed in that cave anyway. I just hope your friend finds his way out of there. Amir, did you say his name was?'

'Yes, I couldn't have done any of it without him. He took me round Beirut and translated for me, he sorted the driver to take us to the caves.'

'That cavern can be dangerous. There are pools and fissures and you said that he's claustrophobic.'

'Papa, he is okay. I saw him when we left. He will have gone for help by now.'

'Quite a team, the pair of you, aren't you?'

'What's that?' said Lottie, as a deep rumbling started and the yacht began to shake.

'It must be the engines. I think we are going for a sail.'

Up on deck, the Count was busy making plans. He had sent messages to interested parties before they set sail, informing them about the tablet he now had in his possession.

'The prisoners are secure,' said Hassan.

'Excellent. When we are clear of the coast, we can dispose of them. No one has seen the Professor for weeks and as for his daughter… well… a young girl alone in a foreign country. Such a tragedy. But really, she should have been more closely supervised. I think we know who will get the blame for that.'

'The English Aunt,' sneered Khalid.

'Indeed. Such an annoying woman. I shall enjoy watching her deal with the authorities.'

He clapped his hands and the butler, in his immaculate white uniform, reappeared.

'I will eat lobster for lunch today. Serve it on the upper deck.'

'Very good sir. Will it be lunch for one?'

'Yes. Gentlemen, you are dismissed. You may relax on the front deck.'

'Thank you,' said Hassan and Khalid together.

The Count picked up his papers, a sign that the conversation had finished.

Mountain Peril

Amir wrestled with his captor without success. He was caught.

'Young man, you are coming with me, and quickly if we are to catch up with the Professor and his daughter.'

'Let me go! My father will hear about this.'

'Indeed he will, and he will not be pleased. Do stop fighting. It will be much easier for both of us if you come quietly.'

Amir had no intention of coming quietly and continued to resist his captor all the way to the car parked at the entrance to the grotto.

'My driver will be back for me. He will alert the police when I don't appear.'

'Your driver has already returned to Beirut. Now will you kindly get into the car.'

The man in the cream suit opened the rear door, and before Amir had chance to make a run for it, shoved him inside. Sitting in the back seat, immaculately dressed as always, was Aunt Helen. The man got into the drivers' seat and they set off.

'Allow me to introduce myself, my name is Helen Evans and I am Charlotte's Aunt, but you already know that don't you? This is Mr Monroe,' said Aunt Helen. 'He has been keeping an eye on you and Charlotte for me. Quite intrepid the pair of you, but then I would expect nothing less from my niece. She is an Evans, after all. Although it

235

would have helped if she had taken me into her confidence.'

'Why would she do that when you are working for the Count?'

Aunt Helen raised an eyebrow.

'Lottie heard you on the phone discussing buyers. She knows that you and the Count are selling treasures.'

'Charlotte should know better than to listen in to other people's conversations. One often misinterprets. Young man, I am not, nor ever have been working for the Count. Quite the opposite. I work for M.E.A.T. The Ministry of Earth's Archaeological Treasures. It is my job to stop people like the Count. We have been following him for some time, but he is very cunning and it has been difficult to find the evidence needed to arrest him. My brother has been helping us. He took the post at the University in order to trap him. It was working until he found an artefact so valuable he couldn't risk it falling into the Count's hands. Unfortunately, you and my niece have led him right to my brother and the treasure.'

'She was worried about her father,' said Amir. 'He left her all these clues.'

'Yes, and she is quite the code cracker. Still, we are where we are.'

'My father?' asked Amir.

'Knows everything,' said Aunt Helen. 'He is waiting for us in Beirut.'

The car sped on. Amir slunk down into the seat. *What had he and Lottie done?* They had jeopardised an important investigation and put the Professor and Lottie in mortal danger. He felt sick and miserable. The radio crackled into life.

'Monroe here,' said the man in the cream suit. 'Yes. I will pass that on.' He turned to Aunt Helen.

'They haven't gone to the house in Aley. The police are heading to the marina.'

'Thank you, Monroe. We will do the same, and quickly.'

Monroe pushed the accelerator and Amir felt the car's speed increase. The mountainside flashed by in a blur. Suddenly there was a loud bang and his first thought was that someone had fired a gun at them. The car swerved dangerously close to the edge of the mountain road. Monroe, wrestling for control, turned the steering wheel and applied the brakes. With an horrendous screeching, the car came to a stop with its front wheels dangling precariously over the side of the mountain.

Aunt Helen flung open the back door and threw Amir out of the car, which then lurched ominously with the change in weight. Neither Aunt Helen or Monroe could move, or the car would pitch forward over the edge with both of them in it.

Once Amir had got to his feet, he was able to assess the situation and realised that Aunt Helen had ensured his safety at the risk of her own. There was no other traffic, so he had to think fast.

The café. Yes. He was about to head off to get help when he heard the rumbling of an approaching vehicle, a heavy one. He looked at the car and knew that the vibrations of the traffic could unbalance it. Without hesitating, he ran in the direction of the sound. Rounding a bend in the road, he found himself in the path of an oncoming truck. Very bravely, he stood in the middle of the road, waving his arms frantically at the truck to make it stop. The driver slammed on his brakes and the lorry lumbered to a halt inches from Amir and the furious driver got out, yelling at him in Arabic. Despite his shouting, Amir managed to explain what had happened and led the man around the corner to show him the car. The driver ran back to his truck for rope and very carefully tied it to the bumper of Aunt Helen's car. Another car travelling up the mountain had also stopped, and its two occupants got out to help. The lorry driver slowly brought his truck closer and secured the rope to it. Then, with the people from the car positioned either side of Aunt Helen's vehicle to help push, he began to reverse the truck. The rope tightened, the bumper strained and threatened to come loose, but with the added momentum of the two people pushing, the stranded vehicle was pulled back to safety.

Amidst the cheers of the rescuers, Aunt Helen emerged from the back, white faced, and Monroe evacuated the driver's seat. A quick examination of the vehicle revealed that they had suffered a blow-out, the shreds of the front tyre hanging loose off the axle. The lorry driver lent them a jack and between them they managed to change the wheel.

Aunt Helen offered the truck driver a reward but he refused. Half an hour later, at a much more sedate pace, they were once again on their way to Beirut.

'Thank you, Amir. Your quick thinking saved us. Monroe and I are very grateful to you. I think, perhaps, I may have misjudged you when I thought you were a bad influence on my niece.'

'I just hope that my father thinks like you,' muttered Amir.

The remainder of the journey passed uneventfully, and they arrived at the marina. Amir looked at the luxury yachts lined up along the moorings, all vying with each other to be the most ostentatious. The curved glass-front of the two-storey clubhouse faced out to sea and guests were sat on the terrace drinking wine or cocktails. The relaxed setting did nothing to ease the churning in his stomach. General Haddad and his men were waiting. Aunt Helen got out of the car to greet him.

'I'm afraid, Miss Evans, that the Count's yacht is no longer moored here. The marina staff say that it left yesterday.'

'That is worrying. I fear that my brother and niece are with the Count's men. Could he have docked it further along the coast?'

'It's possible. I have sent a patrol boat to scout the inshore waters.'

'Good. Then all we can do at this point is wait for news.'

'I have requisitioned the first floor of the clubhouse as a mobile headquarters. You may use that if you wish.'

'Thank you General. That is most kind. I believe that I have something of yours in my car.'

'Of mine?'

'Yes,' said Aunt Helen, opening the rear door of the car. A rather sheepish-looking Amir got out.

'Your son, I believe.'

The general stared incredulously.

'Amir! What are you doing with this lady? How often do I have to tell you to stay out of trouble?'

'It would appear that he and my niece have been collaborating in the hunt for my brother. He is quite the adventurer. However, thanks to his quick-wittedness, Monroe and I were saved from plunging over the mountainside today. I am very grateful to the young man.'

The general looked at his son and didn't know whether to be angry or proud.

'Please, Baba. I was only trying to help. I know you told me not to see Lottie after the night of the party, but she was desperate to find her father and I could translate and take her places and organise a driver, and she's my friend.'

'Enough,' said the general, trying to remain stern. 'Go and wait in the clubhouse while I decide what to do with you. Sergeant, escort my son and see to it that he doesn't get into any more trouble.'

A rather stocky policeman with an enormous moustache and a pompous expression, stepped forward and marched Amir inside and sat him in a corner, leaving another policeman standing guard in front of him. A control centre had been set up with sea charts and shipping lanes. A bank of radio equipment on the left was being manned by two young coastguard operators, watched by three of the General's men. A radio message came in and was hastily scribbled down and handed to one of the policemen. He read it and rushed to deliver it to the General.

'Sir, a yacht matching the description of the Count's has been seen leaving the docks. The heading suggests it is making for Cyprus.'

'Then we need a boat. Call the coastguard for their fastest launch.'

'May I accompany you?' asked Aunt Helen.

'Not this time,' said the General. 'The Count's men are likely to be armed, and I can't risk a civilian. Please wait here with my son. I will make sure that you are kept informed of developments.'

'Very well,' replied Aunt Helen. 'But General, please remember that my brother and niece are likely to be on board.'

'I am anticipating that they are. I can assure you that we will bring them back safely.'

With a final issuing of orders, the General and his men climbed aboard the coastguard vessel as it pulled into the marina. Moments later it headed out to sea again, leaving Aunt Helen watching from the jetty.

The Treasure Seeker

On board the Treasure Seeker, Lottie and her father were growing accustomed to the gloom. Being deep inside the hull, the movement of the boat was less noticeable. Only the constant throb of the engines told them that they were still moving.

'Lottie, can you shuffle your chair next to mine?'

'I think so, if I rock it carefully.'

Little by little, Lottie edged her chair backwards until she was in front of her father. She wasn't worried that the sound of the chair legs scraping on the floor would attract attention because the noise of the engines drowned it out.

'Good girl. Let me see your bonds.'

Professor Evans studied the rope as carefully as he could in the dim light. 'It looks like a figure eight double to me. Can you remember how they work?'

'I think so,' said Lottie.

'Well enough to undo it without looking?'

'I can try. It will be like that challenge you set me last summer, to undo all the knots in your study. Do you remember?'

'Of course I remember my darling girl, because you did it. And you beat me against the clock when we had to tie up Mr Button's rope collection.'

Lottie smiled at the memory.

'It was a good summer. We watched the jousting at Warwick Castle too. I think that was my favourite day.'

Professor Evans looked at his daughter.

'I'm so proud of you, Lottie. I'm sorry I've got you mixed up in this situation.'

'It's okay, Papa. Turn your chair around. Let me try your knot.'

Trying to undo a complicated knot in the dark with her own hands tied up was extremely difficult. The rope was thick and heavy, and stubbornly refusing to budge. The coarse fibres rubbed her fingers, making them sore, and the task more challenging.

'Can you move your wrists up and down to flex the rope a bit?' said Lottie.

The Professor did as she asked and Lottie felt the loops slacken slightly. *I need to change my strategy,* she thought. With eyes closed, she began to visualise the knot, which lines crossed and which path they took. Once she had a clear picture in her head she began again. This time she focused on one loop and pulled and twisted it, coaxing the knot apart.

'I can feel it getting looser,' said Professor Evans, 'Clever girl.'

Ten minutes later his hands were free and he was untying Lottie.

'What now?' she asked.

'We find a way out of here.'

Fortunately, the room wasn't locked; the Count's men believed that their prisoners had been secure. Opening the door just a fraction, the professor peered out. In front of him was the main engine room which luckily was unmanned. A strong smell of engine oil filled their nostrils so they had to hold their breath as they picked their way across to a hatch door at the far end. Professor

Evans opened the hatch quietly. White uniforms hung on the walls next to a small bank of lockers. There was a bench seat along the opposite wall where a few stray items of clothing were scattered.

'I think it must be the crew's changing room,' he whispered. 'I can't see anyone.'

He opened the hatch fully, and he and Lottie climbed out.

'I think we should find a hiding place and hope that the authorities are able to track down this yacht.'

'What about the tablet? Shouldn't we try and find it?' asked Lottie.

'We can't just go wandering about the boat. We'll be seen.'

'But Papa, look, there's a uniform hanging up. If you put it on you could walk about, provided those thugs don't see you.'

'You've been watching too many spy movies,' laughed the Professor.

But he took down the uniform and held it against himself.

'It might fit. I'll try.'

Due to the weight he had lost living in the caves, the trousers fitted him easily. The jacket was a little snug, but he didn't look too bad, apart from his shaggy beard and matted hair. Lottie rummaged around in the lockers, found a comb and began tackling the professor's hair, untangling it and making it look more presentable. The beard was much harder to sort out, but with a bit of effort, she got it to look tidier.

'Shoes,' said Lottie, looking at her father's walking boots. 'You can't wear those with the uniform.'

They looked under the bench and in the lockers and found two pairs of deck shoes. One pair were far too small, but the others fitted.

'Very smart,' said Lottie as she looked at the result.

'What about you?'

'There's nothing for me Papa, but I'm very good at keeping out of sight, if you remember.'

'Yes, I do. You always managed to win at hide and seek.'

The sound of approaching footsteps made them freeze.

'Quick, down the hatch,' said the Professor, pushing Lottie gently through as the door opened. A flustered crew member entered.

'Who are you? Where's Ahmed?'

'He was sick. I'm his replacement,' replied Professor Evans.

The crewman looked the Professor up and down.

'You don't look like the usual type of crew.'

'No. I'm on secondment from the Hotel Excelsior. They are thinking to buy a yacht for guests and wanted some staff to have experience of working at sea,' replied Professor Evans, thinking quickly.

'I have no interest in that,' said the other man. 'Can you polish silver?'

'Yes, of course.'

'Good. Follow me.'

He led the professor up to the main banqueting room where a vast canteen of solid silver cutlery was sitting on a sideboard next to a silver tureen and platter.

'The Count has important guests joining us when we dock in Cyprus. All of this must be gleaming. The polish is in the cupboard. You have one hour. Now, where is that boy Saleem? He is never around when I want him.'

The sailor stormed off to find his missing crew man, leaving Professor Evans to polish the silver.

Lottie, who had shot back up through the hatch as soon as she heard them leave, was cautiously making her way up to the main deck of the boat. She had lost track of her father, but as there was no shouting or sounds of a scuffle, she assumed he was still free.

Voices up ahead stopped her. She dived behind a leather sofa just as the two thugs came into view.

'I am going to visit the casino in Larnaca. Maybe I can double my bonus,' said Khalid.

'Ha, gambling is a fool's game. Mine is going to buy me gold, lots of gold,' said Hassan.

'It was very helpful of the girl to lead us right to the Professor.'

'Yes, especially as that annoying English woman had lost the trail. She will be so angry that we got to the professor before she did,' laughed Hassan. 'She was so determined to get her hands on that tablet. It doesn't look like much to me, but the Count is pleased with it. He's put it on display in the main lounge, ready for his visitors.'

'I need food,' said Khalid. 'Let's go and annoy the galley staff.'

The two men made their way below decks without noticing Lottie, who had heard every word. *If I can get to that lounge, I can retrieve the tablet,* she thought. *I really hope Amir managed to get help.*

Although she was unfamiliar with the yacht's layout, Lottie guessed that the main lounge would be towards the rear of the boat where the deck was wider. Because the majority of the crew were busy preparing for the Count's guests, she was able to manoeuvre through the corridors and along the outer deck without being noticed. She took a moment to look out. The sun sparkled off the cobalt blue sea. In other circumstances she would have marvelled at its beauty, today, she just wanted to see a rescue boat, but behind them was only the swirling of the yacht's wake as it powered onwards. A hand tapped her shoulder and she spun around in a panic.

'Papa,' she whispered. 'I know where the tablet is. It's in the main lounge!'

'I think it's more important to find the control room and send a *Mayday* message,' said Professor Evans. 'Can you remember how to operate a radio?'

'Yes, if it's the same as that old thing in the shed at home.'

'It will be similar. We can work it out. Come on, I think it's this way.'

'But what about the artefact?' said Lottie.

'It's no good to us without a rescue.'

Taking her hand, he led her along the length of the yacht and up an outer stairway to the prow. There they located the control room which was manned by two crew members.

'We need a distraction. Something to get them out of there,' said Lottie.

'Get behind that small funnel,' said the Professor.

Once Lottie was out of sight, he knocked on the control room door. One of the crewmen opened it.

'They need you in the engine room,' said Professor Evans.

The man spoke to his colleague in Arabic and stepped out and down the stairs. Professor Evans removed his jacket and entered the control room. Before the captain had time to react, the professor had thrown his jacket over his head, pulled him to the ground and sat on him. The captain fought back but Professor Evans held firm. Lottie dashed in and scanned the controls. So many buttons and dials on the panel confused her for a few moments. At the far end was a microphone, so she moved towards that. In front of her were three black switches and a dial. The first switch she flicked operated the ship's tannoy and a pre-recorded announcement was played.

'This is your Captain. Welcome to the Treasure Seeker.'

Lottie flicked it off quickly. The second switch brought the radio crackling into life.

'I think that's it,' said Professor Evans. 'Quickly!'

Holding the switch down, Lottie began speaking into the microphone.

'Mayday. Mayday! This is the yacht Treasure Seeker. My name is Lottie Evans. My father and I are being held hostage. May...'

Before she finished, Hassan and Khalid burst in and seized her and the Professor, dragging them back out onto the deck. Lottie was so angry she bit Khalid on his arm, causing him to loosen his grip just enough for her to wriggle free. She sprinted along the deck and hid behind a life raft. Khalid came running, but he didn't see her. Quickly grabbing a length of rope, Lottie looped it around the deck rail and snaked it across the floor. Khalid, realising that he had missed his prey, turned and ran back. At precisely the right moment, Lottie pulled on the rope, creating a trip wire which Khalid went tumbling over swearing loudly in Arabic. He crashed to the floor, hitting his head so hard that he was knocked unconscious.

Without hesitation, Lottie sprinted for the main lounge, the sound of her father struggling with Hassan audible from the other side of the yacht. The Count, aware from the shouting that something was amiss, emerged on deck. While he was distracted by the noise, Lottie seized the opportunity to sneak down the small stairway and into the lounge. There at the far end, in a glass display case, was the tablet her father had found. Seizing a napkin from a champagne cooler, she opened the case and carefully wrapped the fragile object inside the cloth, then made her way very carefully back up on deck.

Overboard

She didn't really have a clear idea of what she was going to do with the tablet, she just wanted to keep it away from the Count. The solution presented itself in the form of a lifeboat on deck. *Perfect*, thought Lottie, lifting the canvas and very gently laying the tile in the bottom of the boat. There was barely time to re-secure the cover before Khalid, having regained consciousness, came along the deck.

Although Lottie ran hard, Khalid's longer strides soon caught up with her and she was once again held in his grip. Making sure to keep his arms a safe distance from her mouth, he carried her kicking and screaming back to the Count.

'You again,' said Count Zindani. 'I have exhausted my patience with the two of you. I think that it is time you were disposed of. Take them away and throw them overboard.'

'No! No! Not my daughter. Please, please. She's just a child!' cried Professor Evans. 'You can't do this. Let her go!'

'It's too late for that, Professor. You should have left her in England.'

'If you throw me overboard you won't know where I've hidden the tablet!' cried Lottie defiantly 'How will that look to your buyers?'

The Count rounded on her, eyes blazing.

'Wait here, Khalid.'

Count Zindani stormed into the main lounge where the glass case stood empty. Howling with rage, he marched up to Lottie and struck her hard across the cheek. The Professor wrestled with his captor, desperate to protect his daughter.

'Leave her alone or I'll… I'll…'

'You'll what, Professor?' said the Count, scornfully.

He turned back to Lottie.

'That is my property. What have you done with it, you little thief?'

'You're the thief,' replied Lottie, eyes stinging from the blow.

'Tell me where it is, or your father goes overboard.'

Professor Evans looked at his daughter. 'Say nothing, Lottie. I love you. I'm so sorry.'

'I love you too, Papa.'

Hassan hauled the Professor towards the rear of the yacht and the little gate for boarding. He undid the bolt and opened it.

'Last chance, or Papa takes a swim.'

Lottie looked from her father to the Count.

'I'm sorry Papa, I can't let him do this to you! It's in the lifeboat.'

The Count nodded smugly to the crewman who had accompanied Hassan and he ran off to check the boat. A few moments later he reappeared with the tablet in his hand. Count Zindani held it up triumphantly.

Then several things happened at once.

A voice boomed out through a loud hailer: 'This is the police. Please bring your vessel to a halt.'

Professor Evans took advantage of the moment to kick Hassan in the knee, then while he was unbalanced, the professor leant far enough forward to topple both of them through the open gate into the sea. Hassan let go of the Professor in a frantic bid to grasp on to the side of the yacht, but missed and fell overboard. Professor Evans hit the water and went under, resurfacing to find a lifebelt, thrown from the police boat, bobbing in the waves. With a few swift kicks he reached it and grabbed hold. The police launch drew up alongside the Treasure Seeker and General Haddad stepped on board. Khalid let go of Lottie and tried to block his way, but the General was too fast and laid him out with two quick karate moves. A second policeman had handcuffs on him before he could resist.

'It's all over, Count. You've been caught with the evidence of your thieving in your hands,' said the General. 'Cooperate and your sentence will be less severe.'

'You will find no evidence on board this yacht,' said the Count, flinging the tablet over the side to disappear below the ocean.

'No! that is priceless,' screamed Lottie, hurling herself at him. The Count was knocked back onto a settee by the strength of her rage. She was on him, pummelling him furiously.

'That was my father's work. You had no right to do that.'

Lottie felt herself being lifted through the air as the policeman pulled her clear of Count Zindani so that the General could handcuff him.

'Take them back to land and ensure that the Professor is brought safely on board.'

'Yes Sir,' said the policeman, leading the Count and Khalid onto the police launch.

The plaintive cries of Hassan could be heard from the water. Someone threw him a rope. Several more police and coastguard officers boarded Treasure Seeker. The crew were rounded up and locked in the hold, along with Hassan who had been unceremoniously dragged back on deck. The police launch, with Professor Evans on board, turned and sped back to shore. The coastguard's men took command of the yacht, turned her around and headed back to Beirut.

'Well, Miss Evans, it would seem you and my son have managed to help us apprehend a major criminal.'

'Your son?' said Lottie.

'Yes, Amir is my son. Did he not tell you?'

'No,' replied Lottie, finally understanding why Amir had called the general a pussycat. She grinned at the memory.

'We do make a good team.'

'You were very lucky. These men are extremely dangerous. My son will be severely punished for placing you in such jeopardy.'

'Oh, no. please don't. It is entirely my fault. I asked him to help.'

'He should have brought you straight to me, or at least to your Aunt Helen.'

'No, no. She is working with the Count. I heard her on the phone talking about buyers.'

The General snorted. 'My dear young lady, your Aunt works for M.E.A.T. the Ministry of Earth's Archaeological Treasures. She is a highly skilled agent and has tracked down many missing artefacts and helped to arrest some major criminals.'

Lottie's jaw dropped open. 'Aunt Helen? Are you sure?'

'Quite sure. We have been working with her and your father for nearly two years in a bid to catch the Count. He is, as you would say, a slippery customer.'

Lottie was trying hard to take all this in. 'Aunt Helen,' she kept repeating. 'Aunt Helen.'

Once on dry land, the Count and Khalid were whisked away in police cars and the Professor was reunited with his sister.

'Christopher, my dear. Good to see you,' said Aunt Helen stiffly.

'Helen,' smiled Professor Evans, then embraced her in the biggest bear hug he could manage. Aunt Helen's initial reaction was to resist and remain as stiff and upright as possible, but her brother held her so long that she finally responded and hugged him back.

When the Treasure Seeker docked, Hassan was taken away to the police headquarters. Lottie was taken to the clubhouse where she found her father and aunt laughing and joking like children.

'Lottie, Lottie, my darling, come and join us. Here, sit down, let me get you a fresh lemonade. The police said they will take our statements later.'

After hugging his daughter, Professor Evans approached the bar to order her a drink and a sandwich. As her father left them, Lottie spoke to Aunt Helen.

'Aunt Helen, I'm so very sorry. I misjudged you. I should have confided in you. It's just that you were always so serious! And you kept having dinner with the Count. Then I heard you on the phone talking about buyers and I'd seen the Count's list, so I thought you were in league with him,' blurted out Lottie. 'And you never told me anything about working with Papa and so...'

'My dear Charlotte,' said Aunt Helen, interrupting her niece mid-flow. 'I am serious because I have a serious job. I didn't talk to you because I didn't want you involved. I had hoped that you would just be able to enjoy being on holiday. It seems I underestimated you, too. I should have known better.'

Lottie smiled awkwardly.

'It was very clever of you to work out my brother's clues, although you did rather slow me down.'

'Slow you down?' said Lottie.

'Yes, my dear,' smiled Aunt Helen, opening her attaché case and producing her own copy of *The Little Grey Men*. 'I don't think your father expected you to be with me when he left the sphinx.'

'That was for you! But I thought he'd left it for me. We use it at home.'

'So did we, when we were growing up.'

'I didn't know that,' said Lottie.

'There is a lot that you don't know, my dear girl. A lot.'

'Amir helped me with all of it, especially translating and finding a driver,' said Lottie. 'Where is he? The General said he would be punished, but he was only helping me. If anyone should be punished it's me.'

Lottie was interrupted by the clubhouse doors opening and the man in the cream suit entering.

'Aunt Helen, he's been following me ever since we arrived,' whispered Lottie, shifting a little closer to her Aunt.

'My dear Charlotte, allow me to introduce Mr Monroe from the ministry. And yes, he has been following you, at my instruction. I had to make sure that someone kept an eye on you, even if you did make it as difficult as possible for him.'

'Pleased to meet at last. George Monroe,' said the man. Lottie shook his hand.

'It seems that I have misjudged most people this summer,' said Lottie.

'Nonsense, my darling,' said Professor Evans, returning with her drink and sandwich. 'You behaved very wisely under the circumstances. Strange country, strange situation. I'd have behaved exactly the same.'

'Thanks, Papa.'

Lottie drank her lemonade and was about to tuck into the sandwich when the clubhouse doors opened again and in walked General Haddad followed by…

'Amir!' yelled Lottie.

He looked at his father, who nodded and the two friends ran to each other and danced delightedly around the room, as they filled each other in on the details of their adventures.

An hour later, with all reunions complete, Lottie and her family were escorted by the General to the Police Headquarters. There they gave full statements about the find, the clues and the kidnapping. Finally, they were taken back to The Excelsior, where they ordered room service. The Professor showered, shaved and changed, then sat with his daughter and sister eating supper, before collapsing, exhausted into bed, Lottie beside him.

Celebrations

A few days later, in one of the smartest restaurants in Beirut, Lottie, Professor Evans, Aunt Helen, General Haddad and Amir, were all sitting enjoying the best Lebanese cuisine. Lottie smiled at the assembled company. Amir was on one side of her, and her father on the other. The general was looking relaxed, and even Aunt Helen had switched her usual black clothes for a rather stylish dark green trouser suit. Thankfully, now that her Papa was back, there was no white and pink lace for Lottie, just a simple, blue linen shirt and white trousers.

'No dress tonight?' grinned Amir, for which remark, Lottie punched his arm.

'Definitely not,' said Lottie.

'I am pleased to announce,' said the General, 'that raids on the Count's warehouses and mansion have yielded many treasures, including the missing items from your dig, Professor. Some of these items were legitimately owned by the Count, but many, many more were stolen from museums or historical sites. He was some kind of middle man. Buyers placed orders with him and then he sourced the items from third parties. My friends, we have stopped a massive criminal organisation. Well done, and thank you. I toast you all.'

The General raised his champagne glass, as did Aunt Helen and Professor Evans. Lottie and Amir raised their lemonades.

'And in case you have not heard,' he continued. 'England won the World Cup.'

'Hooray,' cheered Lottie. 'Well done England.'

'This has turned out to be a very good summer,' said Professor Evans, smiling at his daughter.

'A toast to Lebanon!' cried Lottie.

'Lebanon,' said the others in unison, and clinked glasses.

'I too, have some news,' said Professor Evans. 'Now that the Count has been caught, I have resigned my post at the University and I will be coming home.'

'Papa!' shrieked Lottie. 'Really? But what about your work with Phoenician hieroglyphs?'

'I'm afraid that without the tablet there is little more that I can achieve here. The hieroglyphs will remain unsolved for now. I will be resuming my position at Warwick University.'

Lottie couldn't hide her delight.

'Does that mean weekend visits and days out and Christmas and Easter at home? And Aunt Helen, you must come for Christmas. We'll have such fun.'

'Yes, yes, all of that, darling girl.'

'When do we go home?' asked Lottie.

'You don't go back for another two weeks. We are going to enjoy the sights of Lebanon together,' said Professor Evans.

'Can Amir come with us?'

'Naturally,' said Professor Evans. 'That is, if General Haddad doesn't mind.'

'Not at all. He will get into far less trouble with you than if he is left to his own devices.'

A delighted Amir squeezed Lottie's hand. 'There are so many places to show you. We'll have such an adventure.'

'Another one,' laughed Lottie. 'As long as we are not followed, kidnapped or threatened with drowning.'

Author's Note

This story came to me complete on the plane to Lebanon in 2018, as I watched the videos of places of interest in that wonderful country. Many I had visited before and I realised what a marvellous setting it would make. I scribbled down the plot and outlined my characters, so by the time we landed I was good to go. I set the novel in the 1960's because Beirut at that time was a really cool place for the rich and famous to visit and long before the country suffered the tragedy of civil war. Also, I wanted to write a story that didn't involve modern technology.

A few days into my visit, whilst at the hairdressers, I was handed a large book of photographs of Lebanon in the 60's and 70's. I knew then that I was meant to write this story. The book was a brilliant resource. The hotels, the book shop, cinema etc that feature in the story were all there in its pages, allowing me to give a proper authenticity to the Beirut in my book.

We had gone back to Beirut for our niece, Mahnaz's graduation. When I told her about my story, she made sure that we visited all the places in the book and was just the most amazing guide. I would have liked to have included the ruins at Baalbek, which are so dramatic, but I couldn't work out a feasible way to get my heroine there. Without doubt though, my favourite place and the most truly awesome is Jeita Grotto. Check out the images on the internet.

Lebanon is a brilliant, baffling and wonderful country, full of outstanding beauty and history. I hope that one day, dear reader, you too may be lucky enough to visit it.

Acknowledgements

As always, a huge thank you to my fellow StoryVine members, Sue Newgas, Jenny Heap and Rowen Wilde for their continued support, guidance and critiquing. A special thank you to Jenny for once again sorting out my formatting.

Thank you to Mahnaz Maktebi, for being such a brilliant tour guide while I was in Lebanon and really making my visit the best yet.

Thank you to Alan Sharpe of sharpesketch.com for the splendid internal illustrations and to Leo Hartas for an amazing cover.

A special thank you to Jeff Zindani, for not minding me naming my baddie after him and his brothers. They really are quite lovely and not at all like my fictional Count.

Thank you to my editor, Ellen Morris, for once again offering sound advice and tightening up my prose.

Thank you to my young readers, Shraddhaa Seshadri and Lottie Johnson for their initial enthusiasm for this book.

And finally, thank you to you for reading this book and posting a positive review on Amazon or Goodreads (if you have). I hope that you enjoyed reading it and tell all your friends.

If you want to find out more about my books go to terridaneshyar.com or find me on Facebook.

Works published by Terri Daneshyar

<u>Betty's Bones</u>

Eight-year-old Betty is a fossil finder and dinosaur hunter. When she tries to give her discoveries to the local museum, the Curator thinks she's just a nuisance and sends her away. But when she finds something really special and the Natural History Museum comes calling, things get more exciting than she could have ever imagined…

YA Fantasy

The Light Stone Series

<u>Paladin</u>

Something dark haunts the Shaman-Master's apprentice. Do the Paladin trust him or is betrayal inevitable? A were-spider, a were-snake and an intuitive bowman make up the Paladin, who serve as elite ambassadors for the Shaman-Master. His apprentice Jadeja, leads an ordered and safe life. When he is tasked with leading the Paladin on a hunt for three sacred power stones, the Shaman-Master's only hope to banish an all-powerful demoness, he feels certain to fail.

Protected by sacred runes, they embark on their quest. Dark voices haunt Jadeja and the Paladin don't trust him. They are pursued by a ruthless enemy as Jadeja guides them on an adventure where they battle fearful monsters and face their deepest fears. But what awaits Jadeja is far worse than he could ever imagine… Buy this book to experience this adventure today.

Lamenter

The Light Stone Series

Out of darkness

The light bearer comes.

Vikander is Paladin to the Shaman-Master, sworn to protect him and the Temple of Shang To. But he is betrayed by those closest to him at a time of great danger for the Temple, setting off a chain of catastrophic events. A hidden labradorite crystal opens a portal, allowing demons to attack the temple. The Light Stone, a talisman of immense power, is stolen, releasing a monstrous demoness, and an act of misguided bravery leads to disaster.

When Vikander is called upon to lead the quest to capture the demoness, he doubts that he will have the courage. He must ride the mythical, fire-breathing chimera and survive. Will he and his allies act in time to stop the demoness from making a terrible sacrifice that will tie her to the Light Stone forever?

Printed in Great Britain
by Amazon